To Mo
from Maynard & Susan
They sent Pictures also of The "Hector" Ship. (An Excellent Book.

Oatcakes and Courage

Oatcakes and Courage

Joyce Grant-Smith

QUATTRO BOOKS

Copyright © Joyce Grant-Smith and Quattro Books Inc., 2013

The use of any part of this publication, reproduced, transmitted in any form or by any means, electronic, mechanical, photocopying, or otherwise stored in an electronic retrieval system without the prior consent (as applicable) of the individual author or the designer, is an infringement of the copyright law.

The publication of *Oatcakes and Courage* has been generously supported by the Canada Council for the Arts and the Ontario Arts Council.

 Canada Council for the Arts   Conseil des Arts du Canada

 ONTARIO ARTS COUNCIL
CONSEIL DES ARTS DE L'ONTARIO
50 YEARS OF ONTARIO GOVERNMENT SUPPORT OF THE ARTS
50 ANS DE SOUTIEN DU GOUVERNEMENT DE L'ONTARIO AUX ARTS

Author's photograph: Les Smith
Cover photo: Les Smith
Cover design: Sarah Beaudin
Editor: John Calabro
Typography: Grey Wolf Typography

Library and Archives Canada Cataloguing in Publication

Grant-Smith, Joyce
    Oatcakes and courage / Joyce Grant-Smith.

Also issued in electronic format.
ISBN 978-1-927443-32-3

    1. Scots--Nova Scotia--Fiction. I. Title.

PS8613.R3675O28 2013   C813'.6   C2013-900402-5

Published by Quattro Books Inc.
382 College Street
Toronto, Ontario, M5T 1S8
www.quattrobooks.ca

*For my father,
Freeman John Grant*

Chapter 1

"I cannot," Anne murmured over and over.

She sat atop a craggy hill overlooking the head of Loch Broom. The loch curved and stretched in a sinuous line toward the western horizon. A stiff westerly breeze whipped slate blue waves into frothy whitecaps. Some of Anne's auburn curls escaped from under her hood and she let them writhe, unheeded, about her face.

She asked the wind, "How could Father have promised me to James MacDonald? Even if he'd been deep into his cups, how could he think of such a thing?" The uncaring wind continued on its way.

MacDonald shared the shape and bearing of the great sour boars that he raised. He'd been married twice before and both his wives had died in childbirth. Rumours had gone about the village that the unfortunate wives had carried bruises on their bellies, backs and legs from his hammy fists, and so it was no wonder they'd bled terribly during birthing. Anne didn't doubt the rumours for a moment.

And now, her father had promised *her* to that brute in marriage! To have to keep house for such a slovenly pig...! She shuddered. She couldn't bear to think of the other wifely duties he would expect of her.

If only her mother was still alive, this would never have happened. Mother would not have consented to a betrothal to that horrible MacDonald, regardless of his land or his money or his prize pigs.

She sat and brooded till the sun hung low over the loch, spilling rays of gold and crimson across the waves.

"I would rather die," she declared, her face set and grim.

However, it was not suicide that she was contemplating. A desperate plan, yes. And perhaps fatal when all was said and done. But one worth the risk.

She went home and waited her chance, careful not to let her father see any change in her. She kept to her chores, speaking only when spoken to, and so her father and older brothers paid her no heed.

One summer evening, when Anne's father returned from the pub smelling of whisky and pipe tobacco, he announced, "I'm going to Inverness."

"Oh, aye?" Anne replied.

"Tomorrow. To do some trading."

"Are you going alone?" Anne asked, trying to sound casual.

"Nay. I'm taking the boys with me."

Anne suppressed a smile. With her brothers William and John gone, her plan would be simple. "Will you be gone long?" Anne kept her eyes downcast and her voice even, though her heart was leaping.

"Fortnight. No more. Your Aunt Sarah will be keeping an eye on you, don't you worry."

"I'll pack your things, then. And some food for the trip."

"Thank you, lass," her father said, almost kindly. He peered, blurry-eyed, at her for a moment. "You remind me so…" He shook his head, and bent to pull off his boots. His voice had a gruff edge as he continued. "We'll be having the wedding when I get back."

Anne swallowed the panic that welled up in her throat. She hurried to her father's room to pack his clothes.

Anne wore a mask of detachment as her father, Will and John bade her farewell the next morning, but her heart pounded.

George Grant and his sons had no more than left sight of the farm when Anne threw her cloak about her shoulders. She rushed from the cottage, down a muddy track, and into the tiny village. She hurried along the narrow rutted road, past low cottages, an alehouse, and the butcher's, to the blacksmith's shop.

A bed of coals winked in the forge. Seeing no one within the shop, Anne stepped back outside and scanned about, her hand shielding her eyes from the bright morning sunlight. Coming toward her from the village well, a wooden bucket in each hand, was Ian MacLeod. He was a slim, dark young man, wide through the shoulders, and tall.

"Ian!" she called.

He looked up, and seeing her, smiled. Then the smile dissolved as quickly as it appeared.

"'Morning," he mumbled as he sidled by her into the shop. He set the buckets down, laid wood on the fire, and turned to the bellows. With a practiced rhythm, he fanned the embers. They danced into a sizzling red glow.

Anne followed Ian inside and regarded him, her arms crossed about her waist.

"I guess you heard," she said.

"The whole village is talking of it."

Anne stepped closer and put a hand on Ian's shoulder. "Ian, I do not want to."

His eyes met hers, wordlessly, sad as a hound's.

She repeated, "I do not want to."

"But your father…"

"I know," she interrupted, her voice bitter. "He must owe MacDonald money. Why else would he do such a thing?" Her hands dropped to her sides, clenched in fists.

"Well, MacDonald does have land, and those prize hogs…"

Anne snorted in a most unladylike way.

"When do…When will you…?" Ian stammered wretchedly.

"He expects me to marry in a fortnight."

Ian paled. "So soon."

"I will not marry him, Ian. I'd rather die," Anne whispered.

Ian turned and sat heavily on the anvil, his hands clasped between his knees. "You have no choice, lass."

Anne took a deep breath, letting it out in a sigh. She came to stand in front of Ian, so close that her homespun skirt brushed his knees. "Are you still planning to leave, Ian?"

He looked up at her, startled, confused by her question. "Aye. There's naught here for me. The third son... I'll get nothing. John Ross says I can have a better life. I'll be able to own my own land! I can make something of myself."

"Take me with you."

Ian sprang to his feet, nearly knocking Anne over backward. He grabbed her by the shoulders. "Are you daft? I can't do that!"

"Shh! Don't shout it to the whole village."

Ian was shaking his head and her shoulders in silent denial.

"Just escort me to the ship," she said calmly, as if it were a reasonable request.

"I can't do that. Your father would…"

"I must leave. You can see that. To stay is unthinkable."

"If we get caught, I'll be a dead goose. And you…"

"We won't get caught. We'll leave right away." Her voice was a harsh whisper. "Father and the boys are away to Inverness. They won't know till it's too late. You are going soon, are you not?"

Ian nodded. "On the morrow. I was going to come and say good-bye…"

"By the time my father returns, we'll be long gone. He'll never catch us."

"Lass, do you know what you are asking?" Ian exclaimed. He stood motionless, his dark eyes boring into hers, his hands heavy on her shoulders.

She returned his gaze. "Ian, I cannot stay. I will not stay and become the wife of that … that brute. If you will not take me, then I will leave on my own."

Ian saw the fear and the determination in her chestnut eyes. He swallowed loudly.

"We'll be on the ship before he gets back from Inverness. Then what could he do? Even if he found out where I'd gone, what could he do?"

"You've got me into a lot of scrapes, Anne Grant. But this time... Do you know what you're asking?" he repeated.

She stepped back from him. "Maybe too much." She regarded him for a long, silent moment, then turned and stepped to the doorway. She paused and said over her shoulder, "I am going to leave, Ian. Tonight. I'll wait till dark, so no one will see me go. I would feel safer if it was with you. But I *am* going." With that, she hurried back up the track.

Anne started to throw things into a sack as soon as she returned to the cottage. First, warm clothes and a wool blanket. Then oatcakes and cheese. She found a haunch of smoked pork in the larder, and realizing that it came from MacDonald's farm, refused to touch it.

She hurried into her father's room, to the wooden chest that stood in the corner. She threw a blanket from its lid. It hadn't been opened since they had packed away her mother's few treasures, after her death.

As Anne lifted the heavy lid, the smell that had always lingered around her mother – heather and soap and the salt air off the loch – enveloped Anne. She stifled a sob. She took a deep, steadying breath, and reached inside, moving aside garments.

At last she found what she sought. She pulled out a small emerald-coloured pouch, hand-sewn and embroidered with delicate stitches. She traced a finely crafted thistle with her finger, then parted the drawstring and tipped the pouch. Into her skirt fell three coins.

Her mother had left the money to Anne. That chill March morning, lying in her bed, buried in quilts and blankets, Mother had pressed them into Anne's hand, her fingers as frail as a bird's claw. "If you ever have need," she had said, "it will be here for you. Even though I cannot be." It was the last thing her mother had said to her. The fever had taken her soon afterward.

Anne brushed the back of her hand across her cheeks. She secured the coins back in the pouch and nestled it in her bodice. She carefully closed the lid on the chest and replaced the blanket.

Anne thought about going to see Aunt Sarah one last time, to say good-bye. Aunt Sarah had been good to her, in her own way, and would fret over her disappearance. Anne couldn't blame her for being afraid of George Grant and his fits of temper. But Anne dared not risk the visit. Sarah might just send for her father and foil her one chance to flee.

She ate a supper of cold chicken and black bread and waited for dusk.

Finally, the Evening Star glimmered above the hills. Anne pulled on the best boots she could find – they had been Mother's – and she took her warmest wool cloak. She hefted her bag and left the cottage, closing the door firmly behind her. She gazed out over the loch. She had had many happy years here growing up. But when her mother died, everything seemed to change. The laughter in the house had died with her.

Anne squared her shoulders and started down the path with a determined step. She hoped to reach Ullapool by morning.

A dark form stepped from the cover of a roadside hedge and loomed before Anne. Every hair on the back of her neck stood on end. Anne uttered a terrified squawk, then swung her bag of belongings from her shoulder and spun on her heel, hammering the bag against the side of the intruder's head.

The dark form staggered and collapsed. "Anne!" a voice choked.

She gasped and dropped her bundle. She fell to her knees in front of the prone man.

"Ian!" Anne exclaimed, her voice relieved and reproachful. "You gave me a scare. My heart almost stopped."

"What do you have in that bag, lass? Stones?" Ian asked, sitting up and rubbing his temple gingerly.

"I am so sorry, Ian, but you startled me."

He waved her away and came slowly to his feet. He flexed his neck and shoulders, then peered at Anne in the dim light of the summer stars. Anne picked up Ian's hat, dusted it off and passed it back to him. He placed it very gently on his head.

"So you really mean to leave," he said.

"I do."

Ian nodded and without another word, took up her bundle and placed it over his shoulder. He stooped to grab another bundle from the roadside.

"Ian, I…"

"You have to go, and I can't very well let you roam around the Highlands by yourself, now can I? Even if you are able to bludgeon poor unsuspecting wayfarers to the ground."

Anne's cheeks grew warm. She grinned sheepishly.

Ian continued, "Besides, we're going the same way, seems like. So, there's naught else to say."

Anne reached out and touched his hand. She was so grateful, tears filled her eyes. "Thank you, Ian. I am very glad for your company."

Anne turned her back upon the only home she'd ever known and set off with Ian toward Ullapool.

Chapter 2

THE FIRST HOUR OR so of their journey was a pleasant walk in the country. Anne might have pretended they were out for a midnight stroll. But as the night wore on, the hills grew steeper, the road more rutted and muddy, the wind more chill. Anne settled her cloak around her shoulders and pulled it close.

Ian would not let her carry either bundle, and after they had walked for three hours, Anne had to admit that she was glad. She was having trouble putting one foot in front of the other. The boots were chafing her feet; she was sure she had blisters on her heels. She gritted her teeth and said nothing.

"I am not going back," she thought. "Bleeding heels are a small price to pay for getting out of that marriage."

She let the words "I am not going back," echo in her mind like a chant as she trudged doggedly along the dark road.

Lake Broom lay on their left as they made their way coastward. The track skirted the shore much of the way, although at times they climbed through passes that took them out of sight of the ribbon of lead-coloured water.

Inky clouds blew in and snuffed out the stars. It became hard to see the ruts in the track. Anne began to stumble.

Ian halted when she nearly fell face-first into a puddle. Only his quick, steadying arm prevented a very messy tumble.

"We need to rest a bit," Ian said. He peered into the night. "Down there. We could sit under those beech trees for a while and have a bite to eat."

Anne was sure he could have travelled on all night without rest, but she was too tired and sore to argue. "Aye, that would be grand."

They carefully made their way off the road and down to the grove of trees. To Anne's delight, there was a narrow stream running beneath the beeches. While Ian unpacked some black bread and cheese from his pack, she peeled off her boots and stockings and slipped her feet into the cold water.

Ian sat down and passed her a chunk of bread and a slice of cheese. Then he glanced at her feet. "Ach! Anne, why didn't you say your feet were…?"

"It's fine, Ian. I'll just soak them a bit, and they'll be all right."

Ian took hold of one foot and drew it out of the water. He held it close to his face. "This is not all right. It's a wonder you can walk at all."

"What choice have I got? I have to keep going," Anne said, her chin lifting.

Ian sighed. "Well, we'll have to bandage them before we go on. Otherwise you'll be crawling before we reach Ullapool."

Anne pulled her foot away from Ian's grip and slid it back into the numbing chill of the stream.

They ate in silence. When Ian finished, he brushed the crumbs off his shirt and then dug through the bags. At last, he pulled Anne's spare petticoat from her bundle.

"What are you doing?" Anne asked.

Ian inspected the petticoat a moment, then swiftly tore a strip from the hem.

Anne squawked, "What are you doing!?"

"Making you a bandage. For your feet." Ian ripped a second strip from the undergarment.

"That's my best petticoat!" Anne yelped.

"It *was*," Ian said. "Dry off your feet. Then I'll wrap them for you."

Anne lifted her feet from the stream and huffily dried them on her cloak. She sulked as Ian wound the remnants of the petticoat around her heels. Then he eased her stockings and boots over the bandages.

"How does that feel?" he asked.

Anne wanted to be cross with him. But her feet *were* more comfortable. And he looked so concerned, she couldn't stay annoyed. She sighed. "Better. Thank you."

"Ready to go on? We have about four leagues to go, I think, before Ullapool."

Anne stood. "Aye, ready."

Ian helped Anne to her feet, picked up their packs, and led them back to the road. They climbed a long hill, and as they crested it, the eastern horizon was smudged with a creamy glow.

"Soon be sunrise," Ian said. "It may be raining by then."

They passed sheepcotes and cottages. The wind picked up and began to snap Anne's cape around her legs. As Ian had predicted, the dawn was a wet one. At first, it was a heavy mist, driven by the breeze, but soon it changed to a steady rain, hammering at the right side of their faces. Ian drew his cloak over his shoulders. They ducked their heads into their hoods and tramped on.

Before noon, they came to an inn, The Broom. Its stone walls and creaking wooden sign looked impervious to change or the weather.

"You're soaked to the bone," Ian said. "We're only about a league outside of Ullapool. Why not stop here and dry off? Maybe get a hot meal."

Anne clenched her teeth to keep them from chattering.

"Come on," he said, pushing her through the inn's door. The smell of whisky and ale and tobacco smoke greeted them. A warm fire danced in an enormous stone hearth.

Ian shook back his hood and stamped his feet. "G'day," he called pleasantly to a rotund, red-faced woman behind the counter.

"Nasty day to be out," she said cheerfully.

"It is that," Ian agreed. He took Anne by the elbow and steered her toward the fire. "My poor sister is nearly drowned."

Anne gasped but Ian artfully spun her toward the fireplace to hide her surprised expression from the matron innkeeper and he cleared his throat noisily.

The matron said, "Tsk, tsk. Hang your cloaks up to dry. Would you be wanting a pint of ale?"

Ian hung his cloak and hat next to the hearth, then took Anne's cloak and hung it next to his. He pulled a chair near the fireplace and ushered Anne into it. Then he turned to the woman. "Naught to drink, thank you. But do I smell a mutton stew?"

The woman smiled. It made her wide face look like a split apple. "You do indeed, young man. Would you and your sister care for a bowl?"

"It would help warm us up, I'm sure," Ian replied.

"It won't be but a minute," the woman said and she hurried through a door into the kitchen.

"Sister?" Anne whispered, one eyebrow raised. Ian sat down next to her and held his hands out to the flames.

"What did you want me to say? This is a betrothed lass I'm kidnapping and spiriting away to the New World? She might not have found me so charming if I'd told her that."

"Well, you hardly kidnapped me." Anne thought for a moment. "You could have said you were my squire."

"Sorry, lass. You don't have enough wealth to pull that off."

"Well…"

"And she wouldn't be too impressed if I said we were good childhood friends, either. The only other story I might have tried was to say you were my wife. And somehow I didn't think you would like that tale. You nearly gave us away when I said you were my sister."

Just then, the woman backed through the kitchen door, balancing two steaming bowls of stew on a tray. Ian pulled a table next to the hearth and she set the bowls and spoons on it for them.

"There now. That'll heat you up from the inside out. Where are you going on such a miserable day?"

"Have you heard of John Ross?"

The woman raised both hands over her head and brought them down in a loud clap in front of her ample bosom. "Now who around here hasn't heard of him, I wonder? You're not off to…?"

Ian smiled. "I'm a Scot, through and through, lady innkeeper. And they tell me that in the New World, I'll be able to wear my tartan, and speak the Gaelic, and own land. Now, does that not sound good to you?"

The matron's voice dropped to a whisper. Walls had ears. "Aye. After all the troubles we've had… If me and my man were younger… Ah, but it's a dangerous thing you are planning, my lad."

Ian glanced at Anne as he said, "We live dangerous lives, lady. I just want some choices about the dangers I face." Then he smiled at the matron again. "No need letting the English have a say in everything."

The woman gave him a hearty slap on the shoulder. "Here, now. Eat your stew while it's good and hot."

Anne and Ian ate in silence, letting the food and the fire warm them. The woman returned to her kitchen. The cloaks gently steamed on their hooks.

When they'd finished their stew, the lady innkeeper called to Ian from the kitchen doorway, "Would you care for a piece of dried apple tart?"

Ian licked his lips. "Is it as delicious as the stew?"

The woman giggled in a girlish way, making her jowls quiver. "I'm told it is the best tart this side of Ullapool."

"Then I cannot pass up on that, can I? What about you, sister?"

Anne shot him a glare but said, "Thank you, but I am so full from the stew, I could not eat another bite."

The woman bustled into the kitchen again.

"So, is this the story we are going to keep using?" Anne asked. "That I am your sister?"

"Hmmm?" Ian murmured, his mind on the apple tart.

"Are we going to continue as brother and sister? When we get into Ullapool?"

"I had not really thought about it," Ian admitted.

"Don't you think we should? Think about it, I mean."

The woman reappeared, carrying a large slice of apple tart with a chunk of goat cheese on the side. She stood by Ian's chair till he'd had a bite and rolled his eyes in appreciation. "Delicious. Very good. No doubt the best in Wester Ross!"

The woman went back into the kitchen, smiling widely.

"Is it really that good?" Anne asked.

Ian shook his head. "It's not bad. But it always pays to tell a cook her food is wonderful."

The woman came back into the dining room with a sack. "For your travels," she said. "No extra charge."

Ian paid for their dinner, and as they got up to collect their cloaks, he looked in the sack. There were two pieces of tart, a large chunk of cheese and a small, fresh loaf of dark bread. "See?" he said. "A good idea to compliment the cook."

"I'll remember that," Anne muttered as she followed him to the door.

The rain had slackened to a drizzle and the wind had calmed, but the air held a deeper chill. They hunched into their cloaks.

They had not gone more than a hundred paces when a lone horseman, riding hard and fast, appeared out of the loom behind them. Ian took Anne by the elbow and hauled her between two gorse bushes.

The rider halted his horse abruptly outside The Broom, and left it heaving and blowing, its head between its knees.

"In a great hurry, he is," Ian murmured. He drew Anne further into the prickly gorse.

It was not long till the rider, lean as an alder sapling, came to the door with the lady innkeeper behind him.

"Aye," her voice carried to them, "I'll keep my eyes open for such a scoundrel. You will likely be able to get a fresh horse in Ullapool."

The rider mounted and spurred his horse on. He clattered past Anne and Ian and soon disappeared over the hill.

Ian eased from the hiding place and beckoned Anne to follow.

Anne's face was white. "You don't think he was looking for us, do you?"

Ian looked soberly from the inn to the road. "It doesn't seem likely, does it? And yet, I think we cannot be too careful. At least the dear old soul at the inn didn't let on she'd seen us."

Anne nodded. "Thank goodness you said you liked her apple tart," she said solemnly.

They trudged on without speaking for a time. Their ears were tuned to any sound that might be an approaching horse or a man's step. Anne felt ready to jump at the thrum of a partridge's wing. Exhausted, they eventually came to a rise that overlooked the village of Ullapool – a cluster of low houses huddled on a small cape. The loch was as gray as the clouds, and flecked with white waves.

"Well, here we are, then," Ian said cheerfully. There was a crease between his eyes that betrayed his concern.

"Aye. Is the *Hector* in the harbour?" Anne asked, squinting.

"That's her, at anchor," Ian said, pointing. "See? Three masts."

Anne nodded.

Ian regarded Anne. "Perhaps we'd best sit and talk for a bit."

Anne sighed and nodded. Ian led her to a rock wall just off the road and leaned against it. Anne found a stone at its foot, next to him, and perched on it.

"We've managed to get this far. But I'm not sure how we're going to get you aboard the ship," Ian said quietly.

Anne chewed on her bottom lip. Then she said, "Well, I have been thinking since we left The Broom. I cannot travel as a single woman, can I?"

Ian shook his head. "Nay, and they won't accept that you are my sister. John Ross knows I only have brothers. And an unwed woman aboard… Nay."

Anne looked at the toes of her boots. "Then it seems we will have to pretend to be married."

"Anne, that's…"

"Well, what else can we do?" Her cheeks flushed. "We don't have time to be properly married. Even if you wanted to. And now that we've come this far... Well, we cannot go back. We have to go on."

Ian pulled his hand through his dark hair and looked out over the loch. "I don't know," he said at last.

"No man will ever... I'll never be married now. But I made my choice last night." She peered up into his face. "Will you help me get aboard?"

Ian brought his gaze from the loch to her face. His dark eyes softened.

"You've got me into a lot of scrapes, Anne Grant," he said. "This one makes all the rest seem like naught." He drew away from the stone wall and stooped to pick up their bundles. "But we seem to be going the same way, so..."

Anne bit her lip to hold back the tears. They made their way toward the shore.

Chapter 3

THEY MET MORE AND more people as they entered the village: women with baskets of eggs or wooden water buckets, men bartering or passing the time of day. They passed by an alehouse and heard loud voices within.

Ian stopped so suddenly, Anne walked on several paces before she realized he was not beside her. She turned and raised an eyebrow.

Ian nodded toward a horse, tied outside an inn.

Anne's heart thudded. "Is it...?"

"Aye. See, that's his bedroll tied still on the saddle. He must be inside arranging for another horse."

Anne grabbed Ian's hand and tugged.

Ian moved with her, but his face held a thoughtful frown. When they had gone twenty paces, Ian said, "You get out of sight, Anne. 'Round that shop, yonder. I'll be right back."

"Where are you going?"

"I want to know where that thin rider is going. I'd be most glad to know he won't be sniffing around here all night."

Anne scurried around the cottage at the end of the village lane, leaning against its wall and straining to hear.

Ian sauntered back to stand in front of the alehouse. He tipped his hat over his eyes.

Several minutes passed. Anne willed herself to keep still. She wanted to flee like a startled fawn.

At last, the thin rider emerged from the livery doorway. He stretched his arms and shoulders, then went to the horse he had ridden and removed his saddle and bedroll from its steaming back.

The rider turned to a man who followed him through the door. The other man's back was bowed and his legs were bowed. He looked like he'd been in a saddle from the day he was born. The thin man said to him, "Rode him hard all night. He'll need a good rubdown, rest and feed. I daresay he'll be fine in a day or two. Where is this other horse?"

The bowed man looked at the winded horse doubtfully. "Just around the back," he said curtly. "I hope you don't plan to use him as hard as you used this one."

"With luck, I'll find what I need with little need of more travel."

"So, where are you headed, then?"

The thin man looked down the lane, toward the loch. "As far as my nose takes me."

The bowed man grunted. He stumped forward, and taking the reins of the horse, coaxed it around toward the rear of the livery. He called over his shoulder, "Well, then, you can follow your nose this way to your other horse."

Ian chewed his bottom lip. He waited uncertainly. After a few more minutes, as he was thinking he would learn nothing useful and he might as well return to Anne, the rider appeared on his new horse. He glanced neither left nor right but trotted up the lane and out of the village.

"And good riddance," Ian muttered. He pushed his hat back on his head and hurried to find Anne. She stepped out from her hiding place to meet him.

"Gone?" she asked.

"Rode up and out of the village."

Anne nodded. "Should we go straight to the ship?"

"Aye."

The rocky beach was bustling with men laden with heavy bundles, calling to one another. A pair of oxen hauled a cart to the shingle while seagulls wheeled and squawked overhead. Anne inched closer to Ian and slipped her hand on his elbow.

A short, slight, gray-haired man stood at the shoreline, playing the bagpipes. The melody blended so well with the gulls and the waves, it was truly a song of the sea. Ian stepped over to the piper.

"You are a bold man to be playing," Ian said quietly.

"It's what I do," the man replied softly. "They will have to slit my throat to stop me."

Ian nodded. "I'm going on the *Hector*." Anne squeezed his arm. "That is, my wife and I are going. Do you know who I report to?"

"Aye, laddie. The man you want to see is right over yonder." The piper pointed to a tall man in a frock coat and tricorn hat. "That's Master John Spiers. He's the captain."

"Thank you," Ian said. He led Anne over to Master Spiers.

The master was overseeing the unloading of supplies from the oxcart. He turned to Ian and Anne as they approached. Although Ian was a tall young man, the captain stood half a head above him.

"G'day," Ian began. "I'm Ian MacLeod. John Ross arranged passage for me on your vessel."

"Yes? Good, good. I'll have my mate, Master Orr, check the list."

"Ah, there is one thing, though," Ian stammered.

"Oh?" Master Spiers frowned. He obviously did not take kindly to surprises or complications.

"Well, you see, since I spoke with Mr. Ross, I have… I got married."

"I see," Master Spiers said. "And this is your wife, I presume?"

"Aye. Aye, this is Anne. Anne Grant… Anne MacLeod."

Master Spiers made a small bow to Anne, doffing his tricorn hat. "Mrs. MacLeod," he said. Then he turned back to Ian. "Is your wife accompanying you on the voyage?"

"Oh, aye. I mean, that was what we planned. Is it…? It can be…?"

"Can you make arrangements for her fare, Mr. MacLeod?"

Ian hesitated only a moment before he said, "Aye, sir."

"Well, then. We should have no problem. Master Orr will look after you." The captain hailed a squat, muscular man and beckoned him over. "Take these two to Master Orr. And then get back here on the double. We have a ship to load. Move smartly, man!"

The squat little man stumbled ahead of Anne and Ian on the round, fist-sized stones toward a makeshift table of boards. Without a word, the little fellow turned and trotted back to the master. A beefy man, presumably the mate, sat behind the table. Many sheaves of papers, held down with several of the beach stones, were spread before him.

Master Spiers was a man who was comfortable with his position of authority, and wore it matter-of-factly, like a well-made coat on a chill day. Master James Orr held his power out where it could not be missed, like an over-polished button held right under your nose. He glanced haughtily up at Ian as he approached.

"I'm Ian MacLeod."

The mate said nothing, but raised an eyebrow as if to say, "So?"

"I arranged for my passage on the *Hector* with Mr. Ross."

"I see," Master James Orr said. He looked down at the papers before him. After a lengthy pause he said, "Yes, Ian MacLeod. Here you are. We will be boarding the longboats for the ship tomorrow at high tide. Some other passengers are camping just off the beach, in those trees over yonder. A few have found places to billet in the village…"

Ian interrupted, "I need to arrange passage for my… wife."

Master James Orr's eyebrows disappeared under the brim of his tricorn hat. He glanced at Anne for the first time since they had stepped before him. "This was not arranged with Mr. Ross?"

Ian shook his head. "Well, no. You see, I was not married then." Ian swallowed.

"This does present a problem," the mate declared.

Anne said softly, but firmly, "Master Spiers said that you could make the arrangements for us. We have already spoken to him."

Master Orr glared at Anne for a moment, but when she did not shrink before his gaze, he shifted uncomfortably. His eyes flicked down the beach to where the captain was bawling orders. He looked back at Ian and Anne. "Yes, well, I'm sure something can be worked out."

"What is the fare?" Anne asked, still in that soft, business-like voice.

Master Orr cleared his throat. "Well, full passage is three pounds ten shillings."

Ian's eyes widened as Anne modestly turned her back to them and reached into her bodice. She pulled out the tiny, embroidered bag. Tugging open the drawstrings, she tipped the contents onto her palm – three shiny coins. Anne set them on the table in front of the mate.

Master Orr opened and closed his mouth twice before he could say, "Yes, well, that seems to be all in order. I'll add your name to the list, Mrs. MacLeod. Er… Your given and family names…?"

"Anne Grant."

"Anne Grant. So. That takes care of that. Shall I put the… ah…. Will this go toward your passage as well, Mr. MacLeod?"

"Nay!" Ian said sharply, making the mate and Anne jump. Then he cleared his throat and said quietly, "Nay. I would appreciate it if you would give my… wife what is owing her, please."

The mate scowled but said officiously, "Yes, all right. As you wish. As I said, we begin to board first thing tomorrow morning, and sail with the tide."

The mate retrieved Anne's change from a pouch at his waist. She slipped the coins into the embroidered bag and tucked it back into her bodice. Ian took up their bags and steered Anne by an elbow down the beach. Then he stopped and turned her to look at him.

"Where did you ever get that money?" he asked anxiously.

"Mother gave it to me, before she died." Anne's chin lifted defiantly.

"I would have signed a promissory note, Anne," Ian murmured. "You did not have to…"

"I told you that I just needed you to get me on the ship, Ian. I did not expect you to put yourself into debt for me." Pride made her eyes spark.

"But I would have just the same," Ian said, his eyes dropping to the ground.

His quiet testament melted Anne's heart. "Oh, Ian. You are such a dear friend." She threw her arms about his neck in a quick hug.

He put his hands on her arms and pushed her gently away, flushing bright red. "I feared the mate was going to give us some trouble."

Anne grinned. "He reminded me of Father. A lot of bluster. But when faced with real authority, he'd back down every time. That's why I mentioned speaking to the captain. He would not want to get on the wrong side of the master."

Ian laughed. "Clever lass." He adjusted the bags on his shoulder. "Well, we'd better find a place to settle for the night."

Anne looked up the beach, toward the grove that the mate had indicated earlier. Makeshift tents and campfires could be seen among the trees.

"We are not prepared to camp out," Ian murmured. "We've naught to put over us in case the weather turns foul again." He looked heavenward. "And it looks like it could. Look at those clouds rolling in."

Anne watched the iron-gray, billowing clouds pass overhead. "I don't think we'll find a place in Ullapool, though. With the *Hector* sailing on the morrow, the town will be full. And I wouldn't want to be there if that rider should return. We'll just have to make the best of it."

Ian shrugged, and they plodded up to the treeline. The evergreens were bent from eons of battering west winds. Like tired old fishermen, their branches were gnarled, arthritic limbs.

Little groups of campers huddled under the meagre protection of these twisted guardians of the loch. There were families with small children as well as older couples and single men. As Ian and Anne made their way, searching for a spot to call their own, many people raised a hand or doffed a hat in greeting. A few gazed at them warily.

The trees grew thicker and less spindly as they ventured further into the grove. At last they came to a place that was a little private, under an ancient pine. The blanket of needles acted as a spongy mattress. Without a word spoken, Ian and Anne set their belongings at the trunk of the tree and sat down to rest, their backs against the packs.

After a little while, Ian said, "I'm as hungry as a wolf. What have we left to eat?"

Anne smiled. "Always thinking of your stomach, you are."

They rummaged through the packs and sorted through what food they had. Saving some oatcakes for breakfast, they finished off the bread, cheese, and apple tarts.

Ian patted his stomach and sighed. He flopped onto his back on the pine needles. "This is not so bad."

"Aye. So far."

"Just think, Anne. I'll be able to own land. Mr. Ross says this New World is a paradise. Rich land, plenty of game and fish. Mr. Ross says that any man willing to work will be successful. And I'm not afraid of work!"

"It almost sounds too good to be true."

"But he's seen it with his own eyes. He knows what he's talking about. And just think. I'll be able to wear my tartan! Won't that be grand?"

Anne smiled wanly at Ian's enthusiasm. She was exhausted. Her feet burned where the blisters had broken and bled, and her soles ached as if Ian had hammered on them all day at his anvil. The enormity of what she had done – running away, disgracing her father, and putting Ian's life in danger – settled over her shoulders like a fifty-pound shawl. Her eyes brimmed with tears.

Ian noticed that Anne had become very quiet. He sat up and peered at her in the shadowy gloom.

"Let's have a look at those blisters," he said simply. He hauled off her boots and tenderly removed her stockings and petticoat bandages. His lips pursed in dismay when he looked at the raw flesh under the bandages. He went to work, ripping new strips of clean petticoat and gently wrapping Anne's feet. Then he settled her under the tree, tucking clothes from his pack under her and laying a cloak over her to create as comfortable a bed as possible.

Anne murmured sleepily, "But Ian, what about you? How will you keep warm?"

"No worry, lass. I saved myself a nice warm blanket to wrap up in. Good night."

"G'night," Anne sighed, nearly asleep already.

Ian propped his back against the old pine's trunk and crossed his arms across his chest. He tipped his hat over his eyes and tried to get some sleep.

He must have dozed off for a while because a cold splash of water on the back of his neck brought him awake in a hurry. His head snapped back, smacking his skull on the pine trunk.

It was raining, as he had predicted. "Could I not have been wrong, just this once?" he thought, rubbing his bruised head. The tree was protecting them somewhat, but it was raining harder by the minute, and pretty soon their sheltered little spot was a soggy, cold place indeed.

Anne rolled over and sat up, wiping water from her forehead. "It's raining," she muttered needlessly.

"Aye."

"What should we do now?"

"Maybe if we hang our cloaks on the branches above us, they'll keep the worst of the rain off."

Anne nodded and started to get up.

"I can do this," Ian said.

"I'm sleeping in your cloak," Anne pointed out.

"Oh, aye."

They struggled in the dark, trying to arrange the cloaks overhead. The rain had become a downpour, and they were thoroughly soaked by the time they had the cloaks in place.

"Seems pointless to keep the rain off us now," Anne grumbled. "We can't get any more wet."

"Do you want the rain to keep falling on you all night?" Ian retorted.

Anne shook her head dejectedly, then realized that Ian couldn't see her in the darkness and said, "No."

"Here," he persuaded. "Sit next to me. We'll keep each other warm."

Anne huddled beside Ian. He wrapped his arms around her and they sat dripping and shivering, perfectly miserable.

A soft sound permeated the hammering of the rain. At first, Anne wasn't sure what it was. Then she realized it was someone's quiet, measured step on the wet forest floor.

"Someone's coming," she whispered to Ian.

"Aye."

Anne's heart skipped a beat. Could it be the thin rider? Had he found them? Was it dark enough to conceal them? Or should they run? Anne gathered her legs under her.

A voice hailed them from the gloom. "Hello! It's John MacKay." A feeble light glowed through the trees, bobbing along the trail.

Ian called out, "Over here. We're here, Mr. MacKay."

Anne let out her breath in a relieved sigh.

The light – a small, smoking torch – wove its way toward them. Presently, they could make out the piper's face, eerily lit by the torch's smoldering flame. He held his cape over the smoky torch to keep the rain from snuffing it out.

"I was told that you two had come this way," John MacKay said. "Many of the passengers are getting together, sharing shelter and fire. It's a wretched night, isn't it?"

"Oh, aye, it is that," Ian agreed, coming to his feet, and drawing Anne up.

"Gather your things," the piper said pleasantly. "And follow me. We'll get you to a warm fire."

Gratefully, Anne and Ian collected their few belongings and trailed after John MacKay. He led them to a small clearing where several large canvas tarps had been tented around a welcoming fire. Ian and Anne joined other bedraggled-looking folks who huddled near the fire.

The piper smiled at them. "There, now. That's better."

"Thank you," Ian said earnestly.

"Aye. Thank you so much," Anne said.

"'Tis naught at all," the piper said airily. "Warm yourselves. Once dawn breaks, we'll be off."

Anne sat close to Ian. The warmth of the fire was such a relief after the wet, numbing cold. She rested her head on Ian's shoulder and dozed off.

Chapter 4

THE SOUNDS OF MANY people moving about, breaking camp, woke Anne. She hunched her stiff shoulders and sat up. Ian had left her; his cloak was spread over her, his pack pillowed her head. She blinked and rubbed her gritty eyes. The air was filled with a hushed anticipation and fear.

Anne yawned and drew herself to her feet. She stretched, grimacing, and looked for Ian among the milling men, women and children. At last she saw him striding toward her.

"Have you eaten yet?" he asked as he approached.

"Nay, I just woke. Have you?"

Ian shook his head.

She opened his pack and they sat down to a meagre breakfast of oatcakes. People were leaving the clearing, heading toward the beach.

Ian finished off his oatcake and brushed the crumbs from his shirt. "Well, then, time to be off."

Those words brought back the worry and panic that had gripped Anne the night before. She felt her stomach clench.

Ian reached out his hand and pulled Anne to her feet. "It's not so bad, lass. You'll see."

They gathered their packs and followed along in the stream of travellers headed to the beach. Wisps of early morning mist shifted among the trees, floating like wraiths before them. The branches overhead were heavy with last night's rain, sending cold showers on their heads and shoulders as they passed beneath. They stepped out onto the shore.

At the waterline a queue of people stood or sat waiting for longboats to carry them to the *Hector*. The mate, his face red, his hands on his hips, was barking orders to passengers and crew alike.

Anne and Ian joined the end of the line. Anne gazed out over the loch. The waves were sapphire blue, tossing before a morning breeze. The sun, rising behind them, splashed pale gold and peach light over the stones and water. Anne would have found it quite beautiful if she weren't transfixed by how large the loch seemed. As she imagined the vastness of the sea between Scotland and the New World, it filled her with terror.

What had she been thinking!? She couldn't get on a ship and leave Scotland! It was madness. Her heart pounded heavily. Ian's warm hand on her shoulder was all that kept her from bolting up the beach.

Minutes passed and became an hour. The children became fussy. But no one left his place in line. Anne saw her fear mirrored in the faces all around her. All that held them there, facing the ship and the sea, was the bleak knowledge that there was nothing for them if they turned and left the beach.

A longboat scudded to the shore. Several crewmen held it in place in the shallows as husbands helped wives and children wade out and climb aboard. The queue moved forward. Soon another longboat arrived and it was Ian and Anne's turn. They pulled off their boots and stockings and, knotting the bootlaces together, slung them over their shoulders.

Anne turned to Ian, her face contorted with panic. "Ian," she choked, "I..."

Ian passed one of the packs to a crewman and calmly took Anne's clammy hand in his large, warm one. He looked into her eyes and said softly, "It'll be all right." Then he stepped into the cold waves, gently tugging her along with him. Her heart drumming in her ears, Anne followed.

The salt stung her blisters and the water was numbingly cold as it lapped over her ankles, then her knees. Anne sucked air between her teeth. She tried to hold her skirt out of the waves, but the hem was splashed and dripping by the time she clambered into the longboat. She sat facing Ian.

Rowing out to the ship was not so bad. Anne enjoyed the salt spray on her face and the motion of the sea. A little girl about five years old, with bright red curls and huge hazel eyes, was sitting next to her. The girl started to cry. Her mother was occupied with a babe in her arms and a toddler by her side. She gazed helplessly at the wee red-headed girl, not having a hand free to comfort her.

Anne leaned over to the frightened girl and asked, "What's your name? I'm Anne."

The girl turned to look up at her with brimming eyes. "Christina."

"Well, Christina, would you mind if I put my arm around you? I think it would make me feel better. I've never been in a big boat before."

Christina regarded her solemnly for a moment, then nodded. Anne hugged the child close to her. "Oh, look," Anne exclaimed, pointing, "there's the ship we're going on, the one with three masts. And I think I can see the captain up on the deck. See him? His buttons sparkle in the sunshine. And look at the gulls flying about. I bet they wish the *Hector* were a fishing boat so they could get a meal. Oh, and do you see that cloud up there? It looks like a horse. With its tail streaming out behind."

As Anne chatted on, drawing the girl's eyes here and there, Christina's tears stopped. The girl's mother gave Anne a grateful little smile. Ian caught Anne's eye and winked.

The longboat drew alongside the *Hector*. Anne craned her neck as she stared open-mouthed at the hull looming over them. The port side of the *Hector* rose up like a cliff jutting from the sea, her masts seeming to touch the sky. Anne felt very small. A ladder was lowered and a hoist was provided to aid women, children and baggage aboard. Men carried packs onto the ship.

Anne stepped onto the *Hector*'s deck and was jostled aside by other settlers as they made their way aboard. Passengers milled about, collecting baggage and finding family members. Ian took Anne by the elbow and steered her to a less crowded spot.

A barrage of angry words met them.

"No one sneaks aboard *my* ship. I'll not have stowaways! You are leaving on this longboat!"

"What's this all about?" a broad-chested man with salt-and-pepper hair asked a crewman.

"It's the piper. The MacKay fellow. He didn't have passage spoken for. Tried to get aboard anyway. The captain'll put him off."

Passengers looked at one another unhappily. John MacKay's bagpipes had stirred their Scottish pride. Here they were, going off to the New World, hoping to enjoy freedoms that had been denied them for so long, and this brave piper could not go.

Some men drew together in a knot. Ian sauntered over to join them. Anne could hear scraps of their conversation.

"It's not right…"

"Poor fellow…"

"Something we could do…"

"Captain's a reasonable fellow…"

"His passage…"

The tall, broad-chested man stepped from the group and approached the captain. The captain was escorting John MacKay, bagpipes and baggage, to the ladder and the longboat.

"Excuse me, Captain," the man said. He had a voice like an ox, deep and low. "My name is Archibald Chisholm, and I'd like a word with you, if I may."

Master Spiers regarded Mr. Chisholm coldly. He was obviously very busy, and out of sorts with having to deal with a stowaway. However, he was a man of courtesy, so he said, "If you would be so kind as to be brief, Mr. Chisholm. We have much to do before we sail."

"Aye, of course. We understand that Mr. MacKay here has not made arrangements for his passage."

Master Spiers took a deep, steadying breath. "That is quite right, Mr. Chisholm. I was just now sending him back to shore."

"Well, we would like," Mr. Chisholm turned and indicated the group huddled behind him on the deck, "to have Mr. MacKay accompany us on this voyage. You see, his piping yesterday was… well… it made us feel…" Mr. Chisholm, a sheep farmer from Loch Ness, was not used to public speaking nor to expressing his feelings, poetically or otherwise. Words failed him.

Master Spiers straightened his shoulders. His brass buttons glittered. "I will not have a stowaway on my ship."

"There must be some way we can help," a wiry little man with bushy eyebrows called out from the midst of the group.

Nods and "Ayes!" showed everyone's agreement.

"No one gets a free passage," Master Spiers pointed out.

"Could he not pipe for his passage?" Mr. Chisholm asked. "It would do all our hearts good. Keep our spirits up, like, during the trip."

"Aye, aye," came the chorus behind him.

The wiry man, John Sutherland, called out again, "I would be willing to share my rations with him, if you would let him stay aboard, Master Spiers. It would mean that much to me."

There was a moment of silence, then several more voices called out, "And I would give part of my share too. If he would only play the pipes each day, I would share my bread with him."

Now, Master Spiers was not a stupid man, and he saw this battle was lost. What purpose would it serve to throw John MacKay off his ship? He'd have an angry mob to carry across the ocean. He was out nothing if he let him come. And no doubt, the bagpipe music would help to ease their cares as they made their way across the vast, uncertain miles.

He pretended to weigh the decision carefully, although the scales had been tipped from the beginning. At last he said, "It's your bellies that will be grumbling before the voyage is over. All right. Mr. MacKay shall earn his passage by piping during occasions or ceremonies that are deemed appropriate." He eyed the piper sternly till he received an assenting nod. "And you passengers will be responsible for seeing that Mr. MacKay is adequately fed during the voyage from your rations."

"Aye, oh aye," the crowd assured him.

"Well then, I believe our business here is concluded. If you will excuse me, I have other things to attend to." The captain turned and strode several paces along the deck. Then he spun on his heel and commanded, "Mr. MacKay, you shall pipe the passengers aboard, if you please!" before he continued on his way.

John MacKay made his thanks to the men standing about him. Then he solemnly walked to the rail where another group of settlers was boarding the *Hector* and he began to play.

The ship's deck was getting very crowded as more and more baggage and bodies came on board. Master James Orr, who had just arrived on the longboat, ordered the passengers to move below deck to stow their belongings.

Ian and Anne clutched their bags against their chests and joined the queue to the hatchway. As they waited, they surveyed the ship. They faced the stern and the captain's cabin, which was raised a few steps above the main deck. A pair of low doors was set below the captain's accommodations. Anne wondered what they were for until a young crewman popped out of one. She realized that the crew's quarters must be there. Above the captain's quarters was a transom deck. Anne noticed a pair of carvings at the head of the ladder leading to this deck – the busts of a man and a woman. These carvings looked down upon the settlers with calm detachment.

As the line of settlers moved forward, Anne felt a pang of uneasiness. In the longboat, waiting to come aboard, the *Hector* had seemed monstrous. Now it seemed far too small and crowded to hold all the settlers who were pouring onto her deck. A narrow ladder led to the dark hold below. Ian descended to the hold ahead of Anne, reached up for her bag, and she carefully followed him down.

A lantern hanging next to the ladder cast the hold in a dim, yellow light. Anne's breath caught in her throat. The ceiling was low, and the space was jammed with narrow bunk beds. Cargo that had been picked up in Greenock was stacked, fore and aft, floor to ceiling. Anne surveyed the passenger area with wide eyes. How would nearly two hundred of them ever fit in this cramped space? And the bunks! There were only – she did a quick mental tally – only about fifty beds! That meant they would have to share.

Anne turned to Ian, horrified. She could see by the expression on his face that he was coming to the same realization. There was one bunk bed per family.

Anne looked bleakly at the floor and spied wooden buckets, placed here and there among the beds. "Oh, dear God," Anne thought. "Those are our toilets!"

Her heart racing, Anne spun on her heels and tried to make for the ladder. There was still time to get off the ship. She would go home. Perhaps she could convince her father that she should not be married. Perhaps she could go live with her aunt.

The press of settlers coming down the ladder halted her. She was caught like a sheep in a cote. The air was heavy with tar and damp wood, rotten fish and hot, nervous bodies. Anne's breath came in little gasps.

Ian was at her elbow. He put his arm about her shoulders and said quietly, "It'll be all right, lass. It's not so bad. I can sleep up on the deck. You can have the bunk. And look – see how the Sutherlands and the Chisholms are putting up blankets for a little privacy around their bunks? We can use our cloaks to do that. It will not be very comfortable, but it's better than swimming, eh?"

Anne smiled wanly at his attempt at a joke. She knew Ian was just as scared as she was. But he was putting on a brave face and trying to make her feel better. She squared her shoulders and took a deep breath.

Of course, there really was no turning back. She could never go home.

She heard John MacKay up on deck, playing his pipes. She took heart. She nodded and started to unpack.

Still more settlers poured down the ladder. The air was so heavy Anne thought she would pass out. Little Christina, her two siblings, and their mother were nearby. All three children were crying and the mother's lip was trembling as she tried to hang a blanket from an upper bunk to give her girls some private space. The mother had looked like a sturdy woman when she'd been out on the deck, but here she seemed frail and frightened.

Anne wiggled between other settlers to stand next to the distraught mother. The woman looked at her bleakly. "They are so afraid," she said simply, her voice quivering. She brushed a tendril of mahogany hair off her face, removing a tear from her cheek in the same movement.

Anne nodded. "I'm Anne Grant."

"Katherine McKay MacLeod. And these are my three girls. Hugh MacLeod is my husband. He's up on deck, helping unload the longboat."

"Would it be any help... I could take the children up and let them watch the longboats come in. They might not be so afraid up there. It's so crowded here right now."

Katherine's hazel eyes glistened and she gave a ghost of a smile. "Aye, that would be grand if you would do that."

Anne scooped up the infant girl and tucked her under one arm, then Katherine helped her settle the toddler against her other shoulder. The mother's brow furrowed. "Are you sure you can manage?"

Anne smiled. "They aren't heavy. Come along, Christina, let's go see the boats."

Katherine gave her oldest daughter a little push on the shoulder to get her to follow Anne, and the girl obediently trailed in Anne's wake. It was slow going, but because Anne had the crying babes in her arms, people allowed her to squeeze by, and she eventually found herself at the foot of the ladder.

She hadn't thought how she'd climb up to the deck with her arms full of babies. She stood uncertainly for a moment. A deckhand glanced down and noticed her there. He was gangly, like a half-grown colt, and his face was burned from the sun and the sea wind. He reached down with one long arm and took the toddler from Anne. The little girl's eyes opened as wide as a frightened lamb's, but Anne was up the ladder in no time, and had the child in her arms again. She thanked the crewman, who strode off without a backward glance.

"Probably thinks I'm quite useless, not able to climb a ladder with my arms full. I'd like to see him manage it in a skirt!" Anne fumed.

Once out on the deck, with the salt air blowing in their faces and the boats to watch, the girls' whimpering subsided. Anne set the toddler down, instructing Christina to keep hold of her sister's hand, no matter what. Christina took this responsibility very seriously. The wee girl yelped and Anne had to loosen Christina's fingers.

Christina began to chatter to Anne. "These are my sisters." She indicated the toddler with a tilt of her head. "She's Janet." Then she pointed to the infant in Anne's arms. "She's Alexa. We all got our eyes from Mama and our red hair from Papa."

"I see," said Anne, smiling.

"The crop failure was very bad for Papa. So we are going to find a better place to live across the sea. Mama doesn't really want to go, but Papa said he can't live in Scotland any more, not the way the damned English are using us."

Anne decided not to chastise the child for her blasphemy; she knew Christina was only parroting what she'd heard. It was a sentiment held by most Scots.

The sun was getting high in the sky and the girls were getting restless and hungry. Anne wondered what was going to be done about feeding them.

It looked as if the last longboat was rowing toward the *Hector*. It held only a few passengers.

The captain barked orders. Crewmen swung about in the rigging and bustled on the decks. Anne felt dizzy, watching the men on the masts high above the deck.

Katherine appeared at Anne's side. She had a small loaf of dark bread in her hand. She broke it into four pieces, giving some to the two older girls and offering a bite to Anne. Anne shook her head. "You need your rations," she said. "I'll get my own."

Katherine popped some bread into her mouth and took little Alexa from Anne's tired arms.

"I can't thank you enough," Katherine said, smiling. She had regained her composure and was standing steadfast and calm with her girls about her. The baby nuzzled at her bodice.

"I am very glad to help," Anne said sincerely. "I'm sure we will all need to help one another for the next couple of weeks."

"Aye."

Alexa stopped nuzzling and began to howl lustily. Katherine said, "She's hungry. I'll take her below to feed her. Come, girls. You can finish your bread with me."

The little girls, still hand-in-hand, trundled along after their mother. Anne was put in mind of rose-coloured ducklings waddling after their mother. They turned at the hatchway to give Anne a little wave. She smiled and waved back.

Anne shook her head. She would not want to trade places with Katherine MacLeod, not for a gold crown. Anne had only herself to care for. Katherine had three other precious lives to bring safely to a new land and a new life.

Anne's stomach grumbled. She glanced around. Most of the settlers were up on deck again. Once they'd found a bunk and a place to stow their belongings, they left the oppression of the hold for the sunny topside. A lot of them were eating a chunk of bread. "Where did they get that?" Anne wondered. Just then, Ian appeared. He had a loaf, which he broke in half, passing Anne her share.

"Thank you," she said. "I was getting hungry."

They ate quietly, watching the last longboat as it was unloaded. The longboat was then hoisted from the water, swung aboard the ship, and turned keel upward between the first and second masts. The *Hector*'s anchor was hauled up from the depths of the loch by the windlass and catted up at the bow. More sails were unfurled and the ship slowly turned to lumber down the loch.

Anne gazed at the shore as it slid away, a lump in her throat. She could no longer swallow the bread.

Ian glanced at her tear-streaked face and slipped his arm around her shoulders. They watched in solemn silence as their homeland disappeared.

Chapter 5

THE BAGPIPES HUMMED A sad lament as the *Hector* wallowed over the loch waters toward the open sea.

Except for the orders from the captain and mate and the movements of the crew to keep the vessel steady on her course down the narrow waterway, there was a hush over the ship. All her passengers were overcome by the enormity of leaving their homeland. Parents gathered children close.

John MacKay shifted the bagpipes in his arms and took a deep breath. Then he began to play a rallying song. The rhythm was strong, the melody designed to muster courage and strength. The Scots responded to the call. Backbones stiffened, shoulders squared. The spell of fear was broken. Passengers began to talk softly together.

A solidly built young Scot with deeply tanned skin and a lock of fair hair falling over his forehead came around with a pail of water and a dipper. He resembled a yearling Shire colt: brawny, tall and gangly. "I'm John Stewart," he said pleasantly, with a voice that sounded like it came from the bottom of a barrel. "Drink?"

"Our cups are below," Ian said. "I'll go and fetch them. Do you mind waiting here a moment?"

John Stewart flashed a quick grin. "And where would I be going?" he asked.

Ian nodded and headed for the ladder. The deck was crowded, so he had to weave through knots of people to reach the hatch.

Anne nodded shyly to John. He said, "We get a pint of water a day. And since it looks like we have lots of salt meat for the journey, something to wet our throats is welcome, I am thinking."

"Aye, I am sure," Anne agreed.

"I came aboard at Greenock," John continued. "Passing out the day's water fell to me on the way here, so I have kept on with it."

"I heard there were a few people who took passage there," Anne said.

"Aye. We were delayed quite some time. Cargo. But we're off now."

Ian rejoined them with two wooden cups. John Stewart dipped water from his pail, filled their cups, then with a cheery, "G'day," he moved along to other travellers.

John MacKay put away his pipes and roved the ship, speaking to each group of passengers that he met. He came to Ian and Anne.

"Did you eat?" Ian asked.

"Oh, aye!" John MacKay said, smiling. "Never fear."

"And water?" Anne inquired.

"Aye, my parched throat was quenched too, lassie." His eyes crinkled up as he smiled. "Ah, 'tis good to be off at last." He gazed out over the bow.

"How long," Ian ventured, "do you think the voyage will take?"

"Well now, lad, that be up to God and the weather. And our good ship and captain. But with any luck, we'll be in our new land in four weeks."

"Four weeks! It will really take a whole month!?" Anne asked.

"Oh, aye. The voyages to the New World usually do, lass. Did you not know?"

Anne shook her head.

John MacKay nodded to them both and moved along to speak with the next huddle of passengers along the rail.

As the afternoon wore on, Anne got tired of standing on deck. Her blistered feet throbbed, and the rocking motion of the ship was making her feel light-headed. She thought she'd go below and lie down.

Once she reached her bunk, she realized that she'd made a huge mistake. The air in the hold was heavy with the smell of vomit, urine and diarrhea. Several miserable passengers lay curled on their bunks, moaning or sobbing.

Anne turned to flee to the fresh air on deck when she heard her name called. She swallowed the bile that came to the back of her tongue and turned. Katherine was nearby, stooped over a bunk bed. She beckoned Anne to her.

With enormous force of will over her heaving stomach, Anne stepped up to Katherine. The odour of vomit was overpoweringly sharp.

"This is Janet Fraser," Katherine said, indicating a young woman lying curled on the bunk. Janet's freckles stood out vividly against her pasty white face. Her strawberry-blonde hair was damp on her forehead. "I need you to help me get her out of here and up on deck. Please. I must get her into the air."

Anne clenched her teeth and nodded. She gently took Janet Fraser's shoulders and helped Katherine roll her to sit up. It was only then that Anne realized that Janet was very much pregnant.

"Now," Katherine ordered Janet, "let's get you on your feet."

Katherine and Anne hauled together and managed to bring Janet to standing. She was so weak in the knees that all her weight sagged against them.

"Oh!" Katherine panted, "Come on, Janet. One foot and then the other. We must get you above."

Step by agonizing step, they shuffled toward the ladder.

Anne stumbled and leaned against the upright of the ladder. How in the name of everything holy would they get this woman up on deck?

Just then, Janet retched, and lost what was left of her meagre breakfast.

Anne bit her bottom lip. Her stomach rolled unhappily and threatened to heave.

"What do we do now?" Anne asked Katherine through gritted teeth.

"I'll get Hugh," Katherine said, and she slipped up the ladder before Anne could reply.

"Grand," Anne thought, as she steadied Janet between the ladder and her shoulder. "Here I am with this poor pregnant woman and a puddle of vomit at my feet. Dear Lord, Katherine, don't be long."

Whether in answer to her prayer or because Katherine never lagged about anything, she reappeared moments later with Hugh and his brother Alexander. The two men looked like they'd been fashioned from one cookie cutter. They had the same stocky build, the same solid neck, the same bright red hair and beard.

The men blanched at the mess at the bottom of the steps, but they were valiant enough. They gently hoisted poor Janet Fraser up the ladder and onto the deck. Katherine's husband made a makeshift bed for Janet near the stern out of some canvas and they laid her there. Then the men went off, leaving the womenfolk to deal with the seasickness.

Out in the air, Janet began to revive a bit, but if she opened her eyes to glimpse the horizon rise and fall, rise and fall, she moaned and quickly closed them again.

Katherine went off to find Janet's husband, Kenneth. She sent him to fetch some water. The pregnant woman sipped this thankfully, and finally she slept.

"Now," Katherine said, wrinkling her nose, "I suppose I must clean up below."

Anne swallowed noisily. She knew she could volunteer to sit with Janet and not have to help Katherine. But that seemed cowardly.

She sighed. "I'll help you."

Katherine gave her a quick look, to see if Anne really meant it, and when she saw that she did, gave her a large smile and a squeeze on the arm. "There are many below who are too miserable to move. Someone must care for them."

Anne nodded, not enthusiastically, but with resignation. She followed Katherine into the foul hold.

Several other stouthearted women, Elspie MacLeod (Katherine's sister-in-law), Marion McLeod, Lily Sutherland, and Rebecca Patterson, aided in the cleaning. They worked till dusk, carrying the full buckets out and dumping them over the rails and mopping up the floor. Anne tried to take her mind to other places – heather-covered fields and mountain lochs – to detach from the disgusting chore.

At last, it was so dark, and they were so tired and sickened, they could do no more. They all went out on deck and stood at the rail, letting the sea wind cleanse the stench from their nostrils.

For indeed, they were no longer in the loch, but out in open water. The roll and pitch of the *Hector* was more pronounced, but the evening was calm. The women breathed in the salt spray in silence.

Their menfolk came to find them, and one by one, they drifted off to have their evening rations of salt beef and oatcake.

"Quite a beginning to the voyage," Ian said as they sat with their backs against the longboat. He had polished off his meal in a trice. She was gingerly nibbling hers.

Anne nodded.

"Once everyone gets their sea legs, the sailors say, it will get better. The first day is the worst."

"I pray they are right," Anne mumbled fervently.

"You are worn out," Ian said. "What you have had to deal with these last couple of days! Why don't you go down to the bunk and sleep? I'll stay up here...."

Anne's tender stomach flopped. "Nay!" she exclaimed. "Oh, I could not sleep down there! Please, Ian. Just bring me my cloak, and I'll sleep right here."

Ian's forehead furrowed, but he did as she asked and brought her the cloak and a blanket, and made her as comfortable as possible on the deck. He settled next to her with his back propped against the longboat. Ian folded his arms over his chest, tipped his hat over his eyes, and let sleep take him. Anne's exhaustion eventually drew her into a fitful sleep.

The chill of the morning brought Anne awake, shivering under her cloak. The sky was a leaden gray. Spray dashed over the bow and misted across the deck. Anne felt her stomach rise into her throat as the ship rose and fell beneath her.

Ian approached Anne with cups of water and half a loaf of bread balanced in his hands. He passed the cups to Anne, then sat next to her on the damp deck. Anne pulled the woollen cloak closer about her shoulders before accepting a piece of the bread.

"Did you sleep?" Ian asked.

Anne nodded.

"You look a bit pale. Are you all right?"

Anne swallowed a mouthful of bread and took a sip of water. The food seemed to help settle her stomach. "I think I will be all right."

Ian smiled. "There are many who are not faring so well."

"Don't I know it!"

"Have you enough to break your fast? I gave John MacKay some of our ration this morning."

"Aye. This is fine."

Anne looked out over the opposite rail. "It is terrifying. I don't know how the sailors get used to it."

"What's that?"

Anne made a sweeping gesture with a hand. "Nothing but water. No land. No matter which way you look."

Ian nodded. "Aye. There's no knowing where we are, out here in the vastness of the sea. Gives a man o' the land an awful feeling in his gut." He forced a smile. "The captain knows where he is, though. So we'll have to trust him to get us across this great ocean and to our new home."

Just then, Katherine, one daughter in her arms and the other two trailing along behind, came up to them. "Good morning," she said politely.

"Good day," Ian said, standing and doffing his hat.

Katherine shifted little Alexa from one shoulder to the other and stood with downcast eyes. After a moment, she said, "Last night, once I finally got the girls settled in our bunk… well, there was no room for me to sleep there as well. And I noticed that you had not come down to your bunk, so I thought I'd just rest there until you needed it…."

"Oh, Katherine," Anne said, scrambling to her feet and putting a reassuring hand on Katherine's elbow, "you are most welcome to use our bunk whenever you wish. Isn't she, Ian? I wanted to sleep up here anyway, last night, in the fresh air."

Ian nodded. "Aye, do not fret about that, Mrs. MacLeod. You did not put us out at all."

Katherine smiled at them both. "Thank you. You're very kind. Hugh slept up here, on deck, but I could not leave the girls."

"Of course," Anne replied.

Christina pulled at Anne's skirt. "Let's go look at the Lady of the Ship."

Anne's brow furrowed. "Lady? What lady?"

"The lady up there," Christina said, pointing to the stern.

Katherine explained, "She saw the carving on the transom deck, above the captain's cabin."

"Oh!" Anne exclaimed, understanding. "All right. We will go have a look. Is she very beautiful?"

Christina slipped her little hand into Anne's. "Aye. I think she's a mermaid."

They made their way to the ladder that took them over Master Spiers' cabin. The ship scudded down one wave and lifted upon another in a slow, graceful dance with the sea. From this vantage point they could watch the salt spray curl along the bow and spread into a frothy wave on either side.

Christina gazed at the carving's face for some time. Anne wondered what she saw in it. To her, it looked like any of the women on the ship, the eyes watchful, expectant and wary. Anne glanced at the carving of the man on the opposite side of the deck. His bearded countenance was also familiar; his solemn face mirrored the settlers on the deck. Christina seemed to pay him no attention at all. The "mermaid" held her fascination.

Anne gazed over the deck, then allowed her eyes to lift to the sails billowing above her. They swelled with the brisk breeze, carrying the ship along the waves like huge wings of a seabird. Anne imagined herself as a gull, skimming along the crests of the waves. She raised her arms, holding them outstretched, the sleeves of her frock catching the wind, and closed her eyes.

"You, there!" a voice barked.

Anne's brown eyes flew open. Her arms dropped to her sides. Master Orr was striding across the main deck toward her. Standing at the foot of the ladder, he snarled up at her, "Have you permission to be there?"

Anne replied, "The child just wanted to see the carving..."

"As I thought," Master James Orr interrupted. "The captain doesn't need you lot tramping up there, disturbing him."

A flush of anger rose up Anne's neck and into her face. She drew Christina to her side and she said evenly, "We were hardly doing the Highland fling up here, Master Orr. Now if you will excuse us..." She and the child descended the ladder, and leading Christina by the hand, Anne brushed past the mate, her head held high.

Anne returned Christina to her mother. The little girl's red hair was jewelled with tiny droplets so that she looked like a small mermaid herself. Katherine smiled and hugged her close.

"I suppose there are chores to be done below," Anne said with little enthusiasm.

Katherine nodded. "Rebecca and Elspie have already begun. There are fewer who are sick this morning, I think. People have learned that if they get out on deck, it is better. Only a dozen or so are below."

"Well, that's a blessing," Anne murmured.

The women made their way through the settlers on the deck to do their part with tidying the hold. Anne paused at the base of the ladder and listened. She blanched and turned to Katherine.

"What is that noise? Water running?" she whispered urgently.

"The crew has been manning the bilge pump throughout the night," Katherine replied. Her voice was steady, almost nonchalant, but her eyes were wide.

Anne gasped. It felt as if a hand reached into her chest to squeeze her heart with icy fingers.

"The crewmen say ships always have water that comes in. It's normal," Katherine said in a tight voice.

"Oh, aye?" Anne did not feel reassured.

As Anne went to empty a foul bucket toward the stern of the ship, a round-faced woman lying in a bunk caught her skirt and asked hoarsely, "Lass, could you bring me water?"

"To be sure," Anne said. She hurried away with the filthy, acrid smelling bucket. When she came back a few minutes later she had a cupful of water for the woman.

"Many thanks," the woman croaked before taking a sip. Then she begged, "Would you sit with me for a wee moment? My husband is up on deck. He cannot stand the air down here. It's hard to be here alone."

Anne scrunched herself into the cramped space at the end of the bunk, angling her head so it wouldn't bump into the bunk above. "My name is Anne," she said.

"Margaret. Margaret McLean. Where are you from, Anne?"

"The head of Loch Broom."

A reedy voice piped up from behind Anne. "That's rugged country." Anne swiveled her head in order to see a rather gaunt woman in the bunk behind and to her left.

"Aye," Anne agreed, "but beautiful. I loved to watch the mist on the mountains in the early mornings." Anne swallowed a lump that suddenly came in her throat.

"What I think I'll miss most is the sight of Stirling Castle," Margaret mused.

"It is hard to leave," the gaunt woman sympathized.

Anne blinked quickly two or three times and added, "And the loch had so many moods. It could be calm and friendly or violent and angry, depending on the weather."

"Just like the men of Scotland," Margaret quipped.

Anne and the gaunt lady both snorted. Then the gaunt woman said, "I hear that the New World is much like Scotland. I hope so. I hope it will be a good place for my Jean to settle."

Margaret took another sip of her water and nodded. "They say, Isabel, it's a rough land, but with so much promise."

"I pray we get there soon," Isabel lamented. "The rocking of this cursed ship makes me so ill."

"Would you not both feel better up on deck, in the fresh air?" asked Anne.

"Nay, lass. When I see those waves going up and down, up and down, my head turns to mush and my stomach jumps," Margaret said.

"Would you like some water, too, Isabel?" Anne asked.

"That would be very kind, lass."

"I'll fetch you a cup. Then I'd best be getting on with my share of the chores."

"You're a good lass to stop and chat with us," Margaret said, patting Anne's knee as she rose to go.

Anne was very thankful to be finished with the cleaning and out on deck again before noon.

Passengers gathered in small groups. Most sat, talking. A few sang. One group of men set up a barrel and challenged one another to arm wrestling contests.

Master James Orr's voice carried over the deck. "How is the crew supposed to do its job," he complained loudly, "with such a crowd upon the deck? Why are these passengers not below?" He seemed to be addressing one of the crew. The lad shrugged miserably, murmuring a reply.

Some settlers scowled at the mate and began to make their way toward him. The mate dismissed the unhappy crewman, and turning on his heel announced, "I shall see the captain about this."

Master James Orr strode to the stern and rapped on the captain's door; then he slipped within.

Passengers muttered amongst themselves. They had paid dearly to come on this voyage. They would not be treated like cattle, forced to stay in that dank hold the entire trip.

Moments later, Master James Orr reappeared, leaving the captain's cabin with haughty dignity, his ears red and his jaw set. He said no more about passengers staying below deck. He worked his crew mercilessly the remainder of the day, barking orders and chastising the lads loudly and venomously.

The passengers tried their best to stay out of the way.

Oatcakes and water made the midday meal. Katherine, her girls, Janet Fraser, and Lily Sutherland joined Anne in the lee of the upturned longboat.

The conversation turned to Janet's pregnancy.

Janet said, "I had hoped to be in the New World by this time. But with the ship being delayed in Greenock and all... Well, it cannot be helped. With fair winds we should be in Pictou before my time."

"Of course," Lily assured her with a no-nonsense brusqueness. Lily was a large-bosomed matron with iron gray hair knotted in a tight bun. She had raised a family of seven, and had been a midwife for years.

Anne hoped she was right.

"You have no wee ones yet?" Janet asked Anne.

Anne stared at her, wide-eyed. A red flush rose from her neck into her face. "Oh, nay," she muttered. "I... we... Ian and I have not been married long." The words caught in her throat, making her stammer.

Janet smiled. "Ah, newlyweds," she chuckled.

"How long have you been married?" Katherine asked.

"Oh, ah... only a few weeks."

"Newlyweds indeed," Lily said. "This is not an easy way to start out together. But perhaps you will find a good life in the New World."

Anne nodded. She studied her oatcake, not daring to meet the other ladies' glances.

"Wee ones are a great joy, are they not, Lily?" Katherine said, gazing fondly at her girls.

"Aye, they are a blessing." Lily paused to take a sip of water. Her expression became rueful. "And a trial," she amended.

"Oh, aye. Never a moment's peace," Katherine agreed.

Anne was relieved that the topic had shifted from marriage. She was able to join in the laughter as Katherine told stories of her girls' antics.

A cold rain splashed down upon the *Hector* as dusk settled. Most of the settlers made their way down the ladder to the hold. Anne huddled in the lee of the fo'c'scle as long as she could stand the cold and wet. Finally, the storm drove her below as well.

Anne pressed her way through the many bodies to her bunk. The ever-present stench of sweat and fear and human effluent hung heavily in the cramped space. She took shallow breaths, and made herself busy in the dim light, going through her pack in search of a blanket and a dry robe.

Small children cried out. There were angry words between a couple of the men further forward. Anne could not make out what the argument was about. It would not take much to set off tempers in this crowded atmosphere.

Ian appeared at Anne's side. "It's a downpour out there," he said, not looking her in the eye. "The deck is awash."

Anne shivered despite the stuffy closeness.

Ian frowned, and shifted his weight uncomfortably. "Lass, I can't sleep on deck tonight. I'd drown."

"Oh." Anne blushed, realizing his discomfiture.

There was no question of putting something between them on the bunk. It was barely wide enough to hold two adults nestled closely together. The bunks were jammed so tightly in the hold, it was not possible to even sit up straight in them. There certainly were no spare bunks – some had husband, wife and child piled in together, like packed herring.

Anne looked helplessly about her, then back at Ian. He was her dear friend. He'd risked his life to bring her on this journey.

She squared her shoulders and attempted a smile. "We will have to make the best of it, Ian. There is no help for it."

"I would not put you in such a…"

"Ian," she interrupted. "I put *you* in this terrible position. I made you bring me along on this journey. Now I must deal with the consequences. I know you won't take advantage."

It was Ian's turn to blush. "All right, Anne. We don't have much choice, do we? Where's the blanket?"

They felt very awkward, curling against one another on the narrow bunk, Ian's arm around Anne's shoulder to prevent her from rolling out onto the deck. They were very aware of each other's warmth, breath and closeness. Neither of them got a lot of sleep.

In the morning, they were aroused by a young boy's voice exclaiming, "Look, Papa! It's that easy."

The chatter of a hundred voices dropped. Everyone turned to see who had called out.

It was eight-year-old George MacLeod whose voice had risen above the others. He looked a bit abashed at having so many eyes turn on him. He held a piece of dark wood in his fist as if this explained his outburst.

Mary MacLeod, a petite blond woman, regarded her son with surprise and embarrassment. James, his father asked, "What do you mean?"

Young George swallowed loudly and said in a small voice, that nevertheless carried through the quiet hold, "I was… I mean, the wood came free…"

James took the large splinter from his son's hand and held it up to look at it more closely. It was the size of a blacksmith's thumb and darkened with pitch or tar.

"Where did you get this?" James demanded. He looked every inch of his Viking ancestry, his bushy straw-coloured beard bristling.

George pointed at the side of the hull, next to the bunk where he had been sleeping. "It was right easy. I just sort of picked at it, like, and it came right off."

James peered at the plank that George indicated. Sure enough, the splinter had come from there. And the child was right about the ease with which the wood came free. James scratched at the plank and felt moist rot under his finger. He swore softly. He turned and looked at his fellow passengers.

James was not stupid. He knew announcing his discovery would cause panic to ensue. With his heart thudding heavily in his chest, he said, "So sorry that my son has disturbed you. This is nothing. Please go back to your business."

Mary pressed close to her husband as the other passengers turned back to their own affairs. "James, what do you…?"

"Quiet, Mary. And you too, George." James looked to see that no one was listening. Then he said, "I must talk to Master Spiers. This ship is rotten as dirt. No wonder they have to pump the bilge day and night!"

"Dear God!" Mary whispered, clutching the wooden crucifix at her bosom.

"Do not tell another soul, either of you. We don't want everyone to panic. Try to stay calm. Can you do that, George?"

Young George looked up at his father with wide blue eyes and nodded.

James MacLeod went up on deck and sought out the captain. He found Captain Spiers at the bow, surveying the horizon. The rain had stopped through the night and huge billowing clouds scudded over a pale blue sky.

"A word, please, Captain?" James MacLeod asked.

"Yes, Mr. MacLeod?" the captain replied.

James relayed what his son had discovered, and finished by saying, "Is there not a port nearby that we can make for? It is obviously not safe to continue on this voyage."

Captain Spiers regarded James MacLeod for a long moment. "Mr. MacLeod, it is true that the *Hector* is not a new vessel. However, I believe she is adequate to the task of making this crossing and as the voyage has well begun, we shall continue on our course."

"But Captain…!"

"Mr. MacLeod, I have an obligation to the Philadelphia Company to transport this cargo and these passengers to Nova Scotia. And I shall fulfill that obligation. Good day, sir." Captain Spiers turned and strode to his cabin.

James MacLeod took a deep breath. He sincerely hoped the captain knew the measure of his ship. He himself had little faith in its ability to hold together. He slowly made his way back to his family.

George's exclamation had roused curiosity amongst the passengers. Despite the MacLeods' decision to keep quiet about the boy's discovery, it was not long before several others had picked pieces of the hold away and realized that the *Hector* was barely seaworthy.

Several men visited the captain that day with complaints and pleas to turn the ship around or to head for the nearest port. The captain met with each entreaty in the same way – polite but uncompromising refusal.

The mood on the ship became bleak. Some passengers were nearly catatonic with fear. They expected to go to a watery grave at any moment. Others grew mutinously rebellious. A few placed their faith in the captain and God and tried to go on with the routine they had established.

"'Tis naught but a rotting hulk."

"The company has cheated us. We bought passage to get to the New World. We shall never arrive!"

"We must not think the worst."

"What could be worse?! The captain says he will not go to the nearest port."

"He knows his own ship. Perhaps it looks worse than it is."

"I know rotten wood when I see it!"

"He would not put himself and his crew in danger, now would he?"

"What do we know what a man would do for money?"

"We should force him to turn around. We're only a few days out of Scotland."

"To go back to what, Alex? I'm for going forward, no matter the risks, rather than go back to that life. There is naught there for me now."

The icy hand on Anne's heart returned, squeezing until she felt she could not breathe. She looked out over the vastness of the ocean. A cold sweat trickled down her spine as she thought of the rotting hulk she stood upon. It was all that separated her from the fathomless depths.

Her stomach clenched. Her head spun. She sat on the damp deck, put her head on her knees, and wrapped her arms over her head. Her breath came in small hiccuping sobs.

Ian found her there some time later. He sat next to her and put a warm arm around her shoulders. He did not speak for a long while. At last he said quietly, "I don't believe the captain would risk us all if he didn't believe the ship was up to the voyage, lass. What choice do we have but to trust in his judgment?"

Anne raised her tear-streaked face to gaze into his eyes. "I am so afraid."

"I know. I know." He held her tightly in both arms, giving her something solid and warm to cling to.

John MacKay listened to the frightened talk for a time. Then he took out his bagpipes. He began with a sad, slow ballad. Then he played a couple of rallying marches. Eventually he switched to some rollicking dance tunes.

The music stirred the Scots as words could not have done. The pipes raised their spirits, gave them courage, and reminded them why they were on this journey. There were risks, yes, but were they not off to a better life, a life of freedom?

Lily Sutherland, the large matron, and her wiry little husband, John, were an odd looking couple, so when they got up to lead a few brave souls in dance, there was good-natured kidding and laughter. Others stood around the dancers, clapping their hands. The dour mood was broken.

As he finished playing for supper, John MacKay glanced up at the captain's cabin. Captain Spiers stood in his doorway.

He nodded to the piper. John returned his nod. Then the captain returned to his cabin.

Every day following that, once the morning chores were done, John MacKay brought out his pipes and played. The passengers delighted in singing and dancing to his music. Many days, once he put the pipes away, the men would set up an impromptu ring and stage wrestling matches. The women would cluck at this silliness until it was their own husband in the ring. Then they became quite serious supporters.

The man it seemed impossible to beat was a blacksmith from Beauly, Roderick MacKay. Burly, dark, and with ox-like shoulders, he could not be pinned to the deck.

One day, after a tough match against young Dònald MacDonald, a scrappy sheep farmer from Nairn, Roderick sat and ate his lunch with Ian and Hugh. He finished off his loaf of bread and sat sipping his water, looking out over the endless sea. Idly, he pulled a large iron key from his pocket. Roderick held it in his hand, stroking it, as one might finger a lucky pebble.

He said quietly, "They threw me in jail for having a still."

Ian and Hugh stopped chewing and listened. Roderick rarely spoke, and had never before talked about himself.

"What Scot does not have whisky, I ask you? In Inverness they locked me up. I thought, Roderick boy, they are not going to leave you to rot in a cell. So I made friends with the jailer, see? One night, I says we should have a cuppa together. Sent him out for a bit of ale and whisky."

A small smile played on Roderick's lips. He had a sip of water, wiped his mouth with the back of his massive hand, then continued.

"Well, when the jailer come back, I was behind the door. I stepped out and grabbed him from behind. I snatched the key, and was out the door, quick as a cat. Locked the door, jailin' the jailer. Kept the key."

Roderick caressed the key between his huge thumb and index finger, then stuffed it back in his pocket.

"Hope they had another key to let the poor fool out. He was a decent sort, really. T'was a stout door on that cell, it was."

Roderick heaved himself to his feet and stomped off. Ian and Hugh looked at one another with wide eyes for a moment then burst out laughing.

Chapter 6

THE *HECTOR* HAD BEEN plowing through the North Atlantic for over two weeks. Although the weather had been damp much of that time, the winds had been fair. Life aboard the old vessel fell into a kind of loose routine.

Morning chores were followed by a breakfast of dark bread and water. Then John MacKay pumped up his bagpipes and played for the passengers. Following that, the passengers tended to gather upon the deck, talking, playing games and watching that the children stayed out from under the feet of the crew. Sundays, the captain would lead the settlers in a morning of prayer.

Lunch consisted of salt meat, oatcakes and water. Each settler was treated to gruel made of salt meat once a week. More chores were attended to and then rest time fell over the ship during the sultry afternoons.

Supper was often a repeat of lunch. The food was tedious, but sustaining, Anne supposed. At times, it seemed that the salt meat stuck in her throat, it was so dry. The water did little to quench her thirst. It tasted of moldy wood.

The settlers spent their evenings listening to John MacKay play his pipes or singing the ballads and hymns they loved.

One chill, starlit evening, as Ian and Anne sat listening to the pipes, Ian said, "By now your father knows."

Anne didn't have to ask what he meant. She had thought about her father and brothers every day. Aunt Sarah would have sent for them as soon as she'd discovered Anne was missing. Her father would know that she had run off as soon as he noticed the food and clothing gone. She wondered again about the tall thin rider.

Ian reached out and took her hand in his. "Do you think he'll keep looking for you?"

"Maybe, in hopes of dragging me back for the wedding."

"What do you suppose he'll do?" Ian asked. He looked out over the black, undulating waves, rather than at Anne.

Anne thought for a moment. "He won't want to deal with the shame of me running off. Probably he'll tell people I'm dead. Fallen in the river or something." She gave a rueful shrug. "I may drown yet," she murmured.

"Would you go back if you could?" Ian asked, his voice little more than a whisper.

Anne shook her head. "Nay. I had to leave, Ian."

"You know," Ian faltered, "I had thought… before your father offered you … once I got set up in Pictou…"

Anne leaned forward to peer into Ian's face. He glanced at her, then off into the night again. "Never mind," he murmured.

Anne regarded him for a long moment, trying to read his thoughts, then sat back and gazed at the stars as well.

Many passengers slept on deck, not wanting to endure the stale, fetid air below. There were always ill settlers, confined to their bunks. Family members took turns sitting with them. Lily offered what nursing care she could.

One morning when the wind tossed the waves into whitecaps, several settlers had heaving stomachs. They lay on their bunks, miserable with seasickness. Anne stood forward on deck, letting the chill breeze fan her face as she breathed deeply. As long as she stayed in the fresh air and gazed far out to the horizon, her stomach did not grumble too badly.

Lily Sutherland came to stand next to her at the rail. She said nothing, but stared out over the waves. She held her cloak closely around her. Her face was drawn, her eyes red-rimmed.

Anne put a questioning hand on Lily's shoulder. This woman was usually a brick. Nothing perturbed her.

Lily turned to Anne. A lone tear escaped the corner of her eye and slipped down her cheek. She hastily swept it away with the back of her hand.

"What is it?" Anne whispered.

Lily took a steadying breath and replied in a dull, quiet voice, "Isabel Fraser is sick."

Anne's forehead furrowed. "Aye, she's been seasick since we left Loch Broom, and it's rough today. A lot of us are seasick this morning…"

"Nay," Lily's voice was firm but leaden. "She is not seasick."

"Not…?" Anne blanched. Not sure she really wanted to know, she asked hesitantly, "Then, what…?"

"Smallpox." The word dropped like a stone between them. "She has smallpox."

Anne gasped. "Nay! Are you sure?"

Lily nodded. "Aye."

They stood regarding one another in horror.

Anne finally said, "What do we do?"

"I have told the captain. He asked that she be kept separate from the rest of the passengers and crew." Lily snorted. "As if that were possible, in that crowded hold!"

"Who is caring for her?" Anne asked.

"Myself. Rebecca. Her husband, of course."

"You don't think… oh, Lily…. You don't think others will…?"

Lily gazed at Anne sadly. "In that stinking hold with no fresh air, and with us packed in like herring in a barrel? I don't see how others cannot get sick."

Anne shivered violently and pulled her cloak closer about her.

"I must go back down. Thomas means well, but he is not much of a nurse. Perhaps you could bring me some bread and water in a while?"

Anne nodded, and gave Lily a squeeze on her arm before the matron trudged below to her sick charge.

By noon, everyone on board knew of Isabel's illness. A panic worse than the fear of the *Hector*'s rotten timbers spread like a wave. A leaky boat was one thing. Smallpox among them was silent, lurking, deadly.

A few of the passengers were smallpox survivors or had had cowpox. They volunteered to help care for Isabel and to clean her area of the hold. But many passengers huddled on the deck, refusing to go below for any reason lest they come in contact with the disease.

By nightfall, it was evident that Jean, Isabel's teenage daughter, was also taken with the smallpox. She lay on her bunk, burning with fever. Lily sponged her brow with a wet cloth and prayed late into the night.

Katherine lay huddled on deck, her three girls nestled against her, their blankets and cloaks wrapped around them to shield them from the cold. Her sister-in-law, Elspie, was nearby with her three boys, tucked together like a litter of kittens. Elspie was a stout little woman, with apple cheeks and dark wispy hair.

Katherine whispered, so the girls would not wake, "Oh Anne, I am so afraid. What if my babies get sick? What if…?"

Anne reached out in the darkness and found Katherine's cold hand. She squeezed her fingers.

Katherine held tightly to Anne, like a drowning person clinging to a proffered rope. "They are all I have, my girls. They are everything to me."

"I know."

Katherine murmured a prayer and then fell into a fretful sleep, still grasping Anne's hand.

A hush, like the quiet of a funeral, fell over the ship. Passengers spoke in whispers when they spoke at all. John MacKay continued to play his pipes each morning, but his music was respectfully quiet and sober. There were no games, and any singing was that of psalms and hymns.

The captain made rounds of the sick every morning and evening, offering advice, medicines, and comfort where he could.

Lily Sutherland stayed with Isabel and Jean each night, while Rebecca Patterson and Mary MacLeod nursed them through the days. They bathed the Fraser women's fevered brows and had them drink what they would. Everyone aboard waited and prayed.

Finally, on the eighth day, Mary came on deck and quietly told Thomas that Jean's fever had passed; she seemed to be over the worst. He nodded solemnly, then turned to the rail so others could not see tears of relief spill down his cheeks.

The following night, Isabel's fever broke. She had suffered far more than her daughter. Her age and the weeks of seasickness had taken their toll. But it looked like the disease had run its course and with luck, Isabel would survive.

The passengers heaved a great sigh of relief. The mood on the ship was almost celebratory. Another crisis had come and gone.

Or so they thought. Two days later during a rosy dawn, the settlers were shocked into wakefulness by a cry of terrible anguish. Anne and Ian were among the passengers who rushed to the hold. They found Mary MacLeod weeping and tearing at her hair. Young George lay limply on his bunk, wracked with fever.

Like panicked cattle, settlers backed away and escaped up the ladder. A few men and women went to Mary to comfort her and to offer aid to the sick child. Lily Sutherland's face was lined and grim as she took Mary by the shoulders and gave her a little shake.

"Don't fall apart, Mary. He needs you right now."

Then Lily ordered James MacLeod to bring her water and clean cloths and she sent the rest of the people away.

As Anne turned to go back up on deck, she heard Mary declare, "If I had known I was going to make my boy sick, I never would have nursed that woman...."

Anne tried to stifle her sobs but by the time she reached the deck, she was crying freely. Where would this all lead?

For once, Ian did not seem to have any encouraging words. He stood beside her, his hand on hers, his eyes on the endless ocean.

That day, several canvases were stretched in corners upon the deck, making haphazard tents. Some of the settlers swore they would not return to the diseased hold for the remainder of the voyage, no matter what the weather.

Master Orr bellowed at the settlers to move their messes from the deck. They were in the way of the crew as they were performing their duties, couldn't they see that? Eventually, a sort of stalemate was reached; the passengers found places where Master Orr wouldn't be tripping over them. They huddled anxiously in their makeshift shelters.

The first real storm hit three days later. The *Hector* trembled as waves smashed into her and crashed over her deck. The crew scrambled to take down sails and secure the rigging.

The most adamant settler, who had said he'd never set foot in the disease-laden hold again, was forced below. To remain on deck was an invitation to be swept out to sea.

The crew closed the hatch, to prevent seawater from pouring in, but still, water washed down from above. Crewmen laboured at the bilge pump.

Children cried, sometimes shrieking in fear when the ship pitched wildly down a colossal wave. Mothers held little ones tightly, openly crying themselves. The men fell into grim silence or took to swearing or praying.

Anne and Ian wedged themselves together on their bunk, braced against the tossing of the ship. Anne glanced once through the gloom toward the MacLeod family. James had tied George into the bunk with some rope. He and Mary sat on the edge of the bed, holding a dismal vigil. They found it nearly impossible to even keep a cool cloth on George's fevered forehead. The water bucket had tipped over and rolled away.

With every creak and groan the vessel made, Anne felt sure it would fall to pieces, cracking open like a smashed egg, spilling them all into the merciless ocean. She had nothing left in her stomach. Her heart was in her throat, choking her. She thought she would die of fright if Ian were not braced against her.

The terrifying, pounding night seemed to be never-ending. Anne thought that Hell could not be more horrible, more agonizing, than this suffocating black hold as it was torn and tossed. Every muscle in her panicked body ached from gripping the bunk. At times, she imagined she was holding the rotten hull together with her will and her prayers. She was afraid to close her eyes. Her head throbbed.

Eventually, dawn broke, and with it, the storm abated. The wind died down and the slashing rains eased to a cold drizzle.

The bruised and exhausted settlers slowly made their way onto the deck. Debris from the rigging littered the deck, and seawater crusted everything. The storm had taken anything the settlers had left on deck – canvas, cups, bedding. Whitecaps danced over the heavy swells. The sea was sapphire blue in the early morning light.

They were so seasick and battered from the storm, it was hard to feel joy at having survived. The settlers stumbled to the rails and clung there, breathing in the moist air.

Master James Orr ordered his crew to finish cleaning up the deck and rig the sails. Some of the young lads looked as frightened and seasick as the passengers. Anne had heard a rumour that none of the crew had ever crossed the Atlantic before. Looking at their pale, stricken faces, she started to believe it.

The settlers did their very best to stay out of the crew's way. Archibald Chisholm and John Sutherland offered to help swab the deck.

Gradually, the morning routine took them back into the hold to search for the buckets, mop the floor, and tidy the beds. Several settlers went to sleep then, too tired and sick to eat breakfast.

Anne and Ian went back on deck once their morning chores were completed and had their modest meal of stale bread and water. The sails were taut with wind and the ship seemed to be flying atop the waves.

"Maybe this breeze will hurry us along our voyage," Ian said.

Anne just nodded. She sincerely wished that something would hurry them along. She felt she'd been on this ship forever, afraid forever, and there was still no land in sight.

As they finished their meagre breakfast, they heard the familiar thrum of the bagpipes. Ian turned to face Anne and he gave a lopsided grin. "They still sound sweet, don't they, lass?"

Anne nodded but could not return his smile.

"Do you remember the time we went to Macfarlane's orchard?"

Anne blinked up at Ian. "That was a long time ago."

"Aye. We were nine then. Maybe ten."

Anne's lips trembled into a weak smile. "We climbed into that tree…"

"And ate apples and hung upside down by our knees till the blood rushed to our heads…"

"You filled your pockets and I filled my apron and as we were coming out of the orchard we met old Macfarlane himself…"

Ian laughed. "Aye, he chased us all the way down to Bloody Creek. Wouldn't have got us either, except you dropped your apples and just had to stop and pick them up."

"I wasn't about to leave them, after all that! We thought he would switch us till our backsides were raw," Anne recalled. "But he just dragged us back to the orchard and made us pick apples till suppertime. Let us take home half a bushel too, didn't he?"

"As I remember, it was your idea to go steal apples," Ian teased.

Anne gave him a look of mock innocence. "Me?!"

Ian placed his hand over his heart. "Would never have crossed my mind to do such a thing. You were always getting me into bad scrapes, Anne."

"Hmph. Seems like you didn't need too much persuasion."

Chapter 7

Perhaps it was the stale bread and water. Perhaps it was the gut-clenching fear and seasickness brought on by the storm. Perhaps it was the fetid air of the hold.

By nightfall, six of the settlers took to their bunks with dysentery. Four of them were children.

Mothers sat by their sick children, sponging their faces with water. The hold was quiet. Everyone spoke in whispers. The loudest sounds were the moans and cries of the sick, and the sympathetic creaks and groans of the *Hector*.

The stench in the hold was unbearable. Although the women laboured to keep the buckets clean, the putrid smell of illness hung in the air like a heavy curtain.

The first one to die was poor little George MacLeod. The smallpox took him late at night while his parents sat helplessly holding his limp fingers. James wordlessly bent and kissed his son's cold forehead. Then he wrapped George's body in his blanket, covering the harsh pox-marked skin. James silently walked from the hold. Mary stayed at her child's side, weeping, her face in her hands.

James climbed woodenly to the deck. He found the captain at the bow, a sextant in his hands, checking their course.

James MacLeod said dispiritedly, "Captain, my son is dead."

Captain Spiers put a hand on the settler's shoulder. "I am sorry, Mr. MacLeod."

James nodded once. "Would you be good enough to perform the service...?"

The captain said, "Yes, yes. Of course." He did not wish to upset this good man needlessly, but Captain Spiers knew that having the body remain on the ship any longer than absolutely necessary was a risk he could not take. "At dawn, perhaps?"

James MacLeod looked ready to protest for a moment. Then he simply dropped his eyes to the deck and murmured, "Yes, at dawn."

As James turned to go back to his grieving wife, the captain heard him whisper, "What did I ever come on this cursed journey for?"

As a gray dawn lit the eastern sky, John MacKay assembled everyone upon the deck with the call of the bagpipes. Lily Sutherland's wiry husband, John, and John Stewart helped James carry his son's body on deck. Mary followed, bent with grief, Lily Sutherland at her elbow for support.

The men rested George's body upon the deck, wrapped in a blanket and woolen cloak. When they set the body down, Mary's knees buckled. She collapsed and threw her arms around the shrouded child. She wept, her tears falling on the cloak she had lovingly woven and sewn for him.

Captain Spiers read the funeral service on that still morning in a voice that carried easily over the ship and its passengers. When it was time to commit the body to the sea, James had to lift his sobbing wife from her dead child and hold her tightly. John Sutherland and John Stewart gently picked up the body and allowed it to slip from their arms into the waiting waves.

Mary screamed as George's body hit the water. Then she crumpled in a faint. James held her in his arms, dejectedly watching as the cloaked body of his boy bobbed on the water for a long while before it finally tipped under a wave and disappeared from view.

Three or four of the women wailed loudly. The rest cried quietly into their handkerchiefs. The men, though unaccustomed to revealing tears, had wet streaks lining their faces, soaking their beards.

John MacKay solemnly played the pipes as the settlers and crew gradually slipped away from the grieving mother and father.

Captain Spiers approached Mary and James. Mary had regained consciousness but was stupefied with grief. The captain gave his condolences, then went aft to his cabin.

There was no place for the couple to be alone on the crowded ship to cope with their sorrow, although the other settlers did their best to allow them some privacy, if only by avoiding their place along the railing as they wept.

The MacLeod's loss heightened everyone's sense of dread.

Katherine was nearly beside herself with worry. "Oh, Anne, what am I to do?" she exclaimed.

Anne felt the cold clutch of panic, and fought to keep her voice calm. "The girls seem fine, do they not?"

Katherine nodded. "I think so. But every time one of them coughs, or does not seem hungry, I go cold. I look at poor Mary, and I think that I could not bear what has happened to her."

"I know," Anne murmured. "I know."

In less than a week, that which they feared most descended on them. Five more children were taken sick with smallpox. One of those was Katherine's nephew, Donald, Elspie's youngest boy. Katherine felt a terrible moral dilemma. She felt it was her duty to help nurse her nephew. Would she not expect Elspie's help if their situations were reversed? But she was frozen by the fear that she would spread the disease to her own girls.

At last Hugh said to her, "It is not like you to turn your back on family in a time of need."

It was as if Hugh had slapped her. Katherine squared her shoulders, wiped the tears from her cheeks, and said, "Look after the girls, Hugh." Then without a backward glance, she went below to aid Elspie with little Donald.

Anne watched her go. She bit her lip and looked for a quiet spot.

Later, Anne swept her sleeve across her face as John Stewart approached with his water bucket and ladle. She saw the hesitation in his step and knew he could tell she had been crying.

"Would you like a sip of water, mistress?" he asked politely.

"I don't have my cup with me," Anne murmured.

"I have mine, and I have just rinsed it out, nice and clean." John sat down next to Anne and fished the wooden mug from a pouch tied at his side. He poured, then held the mug out to Anne.

This small gesture of kindness nearly undid her. She blinked back more tears and struggled to keep her face from crumpling. John discreetly looked out over the waves.

Anne regained her composure and sipped the water. John looked down at her face and said, "We didn't really know what we had bargained for, coming aboard, now did we?"

Anne shook her head.

"But then," John continued, "things have been dismal any road. Me, well, I may have starved come winter. So what were we to do?"

Anne nodded. "I suppose we all came because we thought it was better to have a little hope."

"Aye. Although things look bleak here and now, we still have a wee bit of hope."

Anne passed John back his mug. "Thank you, John. For the water. And…"

John shrugged and stood. "My pleasure, mistress."

When the evening meal was served that night, there was much grumbling. The oatcakes were getting stale, and settlers were finding spots of mold on them. Hugh saw people throwing their oatcakes disgustedly into the ocean.

"Wait!" he cried. He rushed over to the rail, stopping a couple that was about to toss their oatcakes overboard. "What are you doing?"

"The food is spoiled," the man said. Hugh recognized Alex Cameron, a tall, dark fellow from Inverness-shire.

"Aye," Alex's reedy wife said, holding up an oatcake to reveal a smudge of green on one edge.

Hugh shook his head. "'Tis a long voyage," he said. "I don't think we should be throwing food away."

"Food!" the wife snorted. Her small, pointed face was pinched in disgust. "This is slops, fit for pigs."

"Just wait," Hugh pleaded.

Hugh hurried to where he'd left his girls. The baby was sleeping on a canvas sack. He gently lifted her and set her onto Christina's lap. "Be a good girl and hold Alexa for a minute." Then he strode back to the Camerons.

Hugh opened the sack and said, "Put your oatcakes in here, if you please, rather than throwing them to the fishes."

Alex Cameron eyed Hugh for a moment. Then he shrugged and dropped the moldy oatcake into the sack. His wife did as well.

Hugh made the rounds of the ship, collecting as many rejected oatcakes as he could. "Perhaps I'm being foolish," he thought. "But we've had nothing but trouble on this voyage. And the idea of throwing away food when there is no land in sight makes my skin crawl."

Collecting spoiled oatcakes became a routine for Hugh. As John Stewart made his rounds with the water, Hugh made his rounds with the sack. Several of the men made snide comments about Hugh's saving ways, but he determinedly carried on.

"If I am wrong, and we do not need this food before all is said and done," Hugh thought, "I will be the happiest man on this ship."

The second child to be claimed by smallpox was the infant girl of Adam and Abigail Murray, a fair young couple from Elgin. Abigail clutched her tiny daughter, bundled in a shawl, to her bosom throughout the funeral. As Captain Spiers finished his prayers, and gently took the dead babe to commit her to the sea, Abigail began to wail. Adam held his wife tightly about the shoulders, and tried to soothe her, but her keening went on and on. Captain Spiers at last felt that he must complete his task, and with as much tenderness as was possible under the circumstances, he dropped the little body into the sea.

It was fortunate that the small bundle remained on the surface for a very short time. Abigail would have followed her lost baby to the bottom of the ocean had Adam not had a firm grasp on her. He fought to hold her as she struggled toward the rail.

John Sutherland and the captain helped restrain the grieving mother. Lily hurried to Abigail's side and between her and Adam, they managed to steer Abigail below to her bunk. There she cried for days, eating nothing and speaking to no one.

The dysentery and smallpox spread rapidly through the youngsters aboard the ship. Their small, growing bodies had the least resistance.

Funerals became a far too frequent event aboard the *Hector*. Anne thought she would go mad if she had to see one more tiny shrouded body slip over the rail and into the ocean. Within the week, they committed five more youngsters to the deep.

Katherine saw little of her daughters as she helped Elspie with little Donald. Anne believed she was avoiding the girls to prevent carrying the disease to them. Hugh was good to the girls, but they missed being with their mother. Anne tried to help entertain them when she could. She took Christina to visit the Lady of the Ship on the transom each day. Anne noticed that Master Orr paid them no attention. He was far too busy to worry over their minor trespass.

One day, as they stood upon the transom, Christina pointed toward the bow. "Anne, what are those?"

Anne peered forward. At first, all she saw was the spray of the bow wave. Then a lithe, silvery body slipped from the sea, arching above the wave. It dove again alongside the ship. A moment later, another appeared, and then another. They resembled fish and yet there was something almost mystical about them.

Anne and Christina watched, enchanted, as the beautiful creatures played in the bow wave, dipping in and out of the sunlight. Eventually, they slid beneath the waves and did not reappear.

"They were mermaids," Christina declared as she and Anne made their way down the ladder.

Anne didn't argue. She would not have been surprised to glimpse lovely maidens' faces on those playful beings.

Sometimes Anne and Christina played with the little rag doll that Christina had brought aboard. The doll often became a mermaid, diving and playing in imaginary waves.

Anne tried to devote some time to the other two girls as well. Janet liked to play that she was a pony, and Anne pranced about the deck with her. She cuddled little Alexa in her arms and made funny faces to make her giggle, and fed her bread soaked in water. Playing with the girls kept Anne from sinking into the dark well of depression that claimed many aboard the *Hector*.

Finally, it seemed that Donald was recovering. His fever broke and he was conscious. Alexander came on deck looking weary to the bone, but with a flicker of hope in his eyes. "He is over the worst now," he announced softly to Hugh, Ian, and Anne as they sat eating breakfast.

Hugh stood and gave his brother a quick embrace. "Ah, that's good news, lad. You look done in. Have you eaten?"

"Nay. I'm too tired to eat. I'll just find a place to sleep, thank you."

Once Katherine was quite sure that Donald was recovering, she returned to her family. It was late evening. The sky was a cloudless navy, pinpointed with a million stars. Fine lines etched Katherine's face and black circles rimmed her hazel eyes. She slumped onto the deck and gathered her girls around her, like a hen drawing her chicks under her wings for the night.

"I've missed you," she whispered. She kissed each little girl on the head, then promptly fell asleep.

After a week, little Donald MacLeod was able to come up on deck. His round face was scarred and pitted from the pox, and he was so weak, he had to be carried. But the two-year-old did not seem to mind either of these things. He basked in the attention given him by the matrons on board, and he laughed joyfully at the antics of his two older brothers. Elspie beamed at her youngest son.

The next week, three more children died in the hold of the *Hector* and had to be committed to the deep. The week following, the smallpox took two more. It seemed for every small blessing, there was an enormous toll of grief to be paid. The settlers wore the haggard, desperate look of animals in a trap.

Chapter 8

ONE NIGHT, WHEN THEY had been voyaging for six weeks, the settlers on deck were awakened by a piercing scream. They sprang to their feet, hearts hammering, eyes wide.

Another scream split the night, followed by a man's voice pleading, "What should I do?"

Settlers rushed forward, and found Janet Fraser and her husband huddled under a scrap of canvas next to the longboat. As men and women crowded about them, Kenneth Fraser whimpered, "It's her time. The babe is coming. What do I do?"

Lily Sutherland pushed forward. "You stop whining like a child for starters, Kenneth. Get Janet some blankets to lie on and to cover her. It's cold." Lily turned to the assembled crowd. "She does not need all of you around, staring at her. Go on! Anne, stay and give me a hand. John, bring water and clean cloths and a lantern."

The crowd melted away. John Sutherland led Kenneth off to find blankets and cloaks. Anne knelt down beside Janet and held her shaking hand.

Lily said, "Now, Janet, I know it hurts. So scream if you must. But try not to scare all the men into jumping off the ship."

Janet gave a wan smile.

"What do I do?" Anne whispered, realizing she was parroting poor Kenneth. She had never attended a birthing before, and she thought she must be as scared as Janet.

"Exactly what you are doing. Talk to Janet. Hold her hand. Remember lasses, this is a natural process. Women have been having babies since God made the earth."

John Sutherland wordlessly set a bucket of water, a lit lantern, and a clean linen raiment next to his wife and slipped away. Anne thought the linen looked suspiciously like what was left of her best petticoat.

Kenneth returned with an armful of blankets. He stood looking helplessly upon his wife. Janet's pale, freckled face was contorted with pain. Kenneth's mouth opened and closed several times, but nothing came out but a few incomprehensible moans.

Lily stood and scooped the blankets from his arms, then dismissed him with, "Now go away, Kenneth. I'll let you know when you are a father."

He shuffled his feet for a moment, then turned and shambled to the stern where John Sutherland, Ian, Hugh and Alexander sat waiting for him.

John patted him on the shoulder as he sat down. "Be brave, lad."

Kenneth nodded glumly and stared across the deck through the darkness. His face was as pale as the moon. He could hear Janet panting.

"Now," Lily was saying to Janet, "you need to rest whenever you can. As the word suggests, labour is hard work. So between pains, take long, deep breaths and wait."

Janet stared at Lily with huge eyes. The contractions terrified her. She had never felt pain like this in her life.

Lily rolled Janet so she could put a blanket under her, then spread one over her. "Are you warm enough?" she asked gently, as to a child she was tucking into bed for the night.

Janet nodded.

"Good. You're sweating and we don't want you to get a chill. Now, let me look and see how far this wee bairn has come."

Anne squeezed Janet's fingers and said, "I guess this baby is not going to be a patient one. It could not wait to get to the New World to be born."

"What a terrible time...!" Janet wailed.

"Nay," Anne hurried to say. "It means it's a good strong soul with a will to be alive. That's a good thing."

Janet searched Anne's face. "Do you think that?"

"Of course!" Anne said with as much conviction as she could muster. "This babe wants to get that first look at the New World with the rest of us."

Just then, a contraction hit. Janet clenched her teeth and groaned.

"Just hold steady, lass," Lily instructed gently.

Janet cried out. Anne felt her fingers go numb as Janet crushed them between hers. After a few moments, the pain subsided, and Janet lay shaking on the blankets.

"You are doing fine," Lily said calmly.

Anne's heart pounded. She smoothed damp curls from Janet's sweat-beaded forehead. Her own hands were shaking. She took a couple of deep breaths. Lily caught her eye and gave her an encouraging nod.

The pains began to come more quickly and finally Lily told Janet, "All right, lassie. It's time to push."

Another contraction washed over Janet. She lifted her head and shoulders with the effort of her push. Anne helped support Janet's shoulders with her arms. Lily called out, "Good girl. That's it."

This continued throughout the remainder of the night. Anne lost count of the contractions that wracked through Janet. Anne was exhausted from helping the young mother-to-be. She couldn't imagine how wasted Janet must feel.

Now, between pains, Janet lay limply on the bed of blankets. Her shift was soaked in sweat. She whimpered once, "I can't."

Anne could see the transom deck silhouetted in the lightening gray of dawn when Lily said, "This time, the baby is coming, Janet. Do you hear me? Give it everything you have. Here we go!"

Anne pressed on Janet's back. Janet sat up and gave a battle cry that would make her clan elders proud. Her face scrunched together in a grimace of great concentration. She bore down.

"Aye! That's it! Push! More! Just a little more!" Lily cried.

Janet gave another great push, then fell back, totally exhausted.

Anne waited. All was quiet but for Janet's panting breath. Then Lily whispered, "Janet, you have a daughter."

The mewing cry of a newborn babe poured over them like warm honey.

Tears streamed from the corners of Janet's eyes. She lay with her eyes closed, a tiny smile creasing her lips.

Lily hurriedly wrapped the baby in a soft blanket and set her on the new mother's heart.

Janet opened her eyes and in the new dawn light, gazed at her baby girl. Anne was weeping and laughing. She looked up at Lily to see the midwife's eyes glistening. They smiled at one another.

"You girls did just fine," Lily said, patting Janet and then Anne on the shoulder.

Lily tidied up a bit, then said, "Now, I'd better go see Kenneth and tell him that he is a father. After that battle cry of yours, Janet, he may wonder what I've done to you."

Janet whispered, "Thank you, Lily. Oh, thank you."

Lily tried to compose her face. Smiles and tears fought to overcome the usual passive calm of her features. "You are welcome, lass. I'll be back shortly."

Lily turned and bustled across the deck.

Anne reached out to touch the tiny infant's cheek. She was delicate and soft as a rose petal. She had a wisp of ginger hair, like her mother's. Anne asked, "What will you call her?"

"Jane. After my mother," Janet murmured.

"That's a lovely name."

Kenneth rushed over and began to fuss over his wife and daughter as new fathers do. Anne excused herself and left them to their happy moment.

Blessedly, Baby Jane did seem to be a strong and willful soul. She had a hearty appetite and a good set of lungs. The passengers didn't even mind too much that she woke them every night with her lusty cries for milk. It was a joy to have a healthy new life among them.

A couple of days later, the *Hector* rocked upon gentle swells as light, wispy clouds skimmed the turquoise sky. Kenneth and Janet, with baby Jane, joined Hugh, Katherine, the girls, Alexander, Elspie, their boys, Anne and Ian for their midday meal. There was a comfortable camaraderie amongst them, and when conversation lapsed, no one felt the need to fill the peaceful silence.

Little Christina's voice carried very clearly, then, when she turned to her father and asked, "Where did Baby Jane come from?"

Hugh's face turned as red as his bright hair. He gaped at Christina. The rest of the group sat for a moment in stunned silence, then a quiet titter of laughter rippled the air. Hugh looked from face to face, aghast.

He gazed down at Christina again. She sat with a small frown puckering her forehead. She didn't understand the delay in getting an answer to her question or the chuckles of the adults.

"I do not think that is a question that you should be asking…" Hugh choked.

"Why?" Christina asked, eyes wide.

"Well, because, it's…" Hugh looked beseechingly at Katherine. She raised an eyebrow, but offered no assistance.

"It's not a question for a young lady to ask in such company."

Christina looked at the people about her. They were all family or folks friendly with her mama and papa. What was wrong with asking a question here? Her confusion was evident in her pouting lips.

Hugh's face grew redder still. Alexander's shoulders were shaking with the effort of controlling his laughter. Hugh scowled at him.

"Baby Jane was not on the ship when we left Scotland, was she?" Christina persisted. "I didn't see her. So where did she come from?"

Hugh threw up his hands. "Katherine!"

Katherine took pity on Hugh and beckoned Christina over to her. She settled Christina next to her on the deck and said, "Baby Jane was on the ship, but you couldn't see her."

"How? How could I not see her?" Christina's eyes were enormous with wonder.

Hugh, still red and flustered, strode off to the stern. Chuckling loudly, Alexander followed.

Katherine explained, "The baby was in an egg. A very special egg."

Christina puzzled over that for a moment, then asked, "Why did I not see the egg, then?"

Katherine smiled. "Ah, the egg was in a very safe place. It was in Janet's belly. It stayed there, safe and warm until Baby Jane was ready to be born."

"Oh," Christina said. She looked Janet up and down. Then she asked, "How did she know when she was ready?"

"God knew," Katherine said. "Just like when a baby chick is ready to come out of its egg. When it's the right time, the babe will come."

Christina glanced at baby Jane, then nodded, satisfied. She hopped up and trotted across the deck toward her father.

"I think she's gone to explain it all to Hugh," Kenneth snorted.

Katherine nodded.

Ian chuckled, "Poor man."

"I liked your explanation," Anne told Katherine.

Katherine winked at Anne. "Maybe one day you will use that little story to tell your own daughter where a babe comes from."

It was Anne's turn to blush.

At suppertime, when John Stewart made his rounds with his bucket of water, he did not have his usual cheery smile.

"Hello, there, John," Hugh greeted him.

"I am afraid I am the bearer of more bad news," John Stewart said glumly, raking one hand through his forelock of straw-coloured hair.

Anne and Ian scrambled to their feet. Now what was wrong?

"It seems," John said, his deep voice toneless, "that the voyage is taking longer than was expected. We have a long way to go yet."

"That is bad news," Ian said.

"And," John continued, "because of that, our water rations may not be sufficient to last out the trip. So I have been told by Master Orr to half the daily water allotted to everyone."

Anne glanced at the crumbling oatcake in her hand. Her throat was parched much of the time as it was, with merely a pint to drink each day.

"Half a pint!" Hugh roared.

"Well," John Stewart said listlessly, "it's that, or have no water at all for the last week or so that we're at sea. That's how Master Orr put it to me. I don't relish that idea at all."

Hugh took a steadying breath. Ian and Anne looked at one another sorrowfully, then Ian shrugged.

They held out their cups and accepted their meagre ration of breakfast water. They sipped it slowly to make it last.

Chapter 9

WHEN ANNE WOKE ONE late August morning, she knew something was not right, even before she opened her eyes. An eerie hush enveloped the ship.

Anne came to her feet and looked about. The sea was as flat as a platter; the rising sun reflected on its surface like a mirror. Anne tilted her head and gazed at the masts. The sails lay as limp as wilted leaves. The *Hector* sat serenely, a dozing swan on a millpond.

At first, Anne felt joy at the calm and beauty of the morning. She didn't have to brace her legs to walk upon the deck. The ocean was enchanted in its stillness.

Then, as she watched the tension on the faces of the sailors and the pacing of the captain upon the transom, she realized that without the wind and the waves, the ship was stalled.

That realization dawned on all the passengers during the morning. "We are stuck here in the middle of the ocean!" Alex Cameron groused.

"Aye." John Sutherland frowned, his bushy eyebrows meeting in a 'v' over his nose. "But there is naught we can do about it. Unless you can whistle up the wind."

"It is one thing after another on this accursed voyage," Rebecca Patterson grumbled, her thin arms folded across her scrawny bosom.

"John Ross made it seem like it was naught but a wee trip to paradise, did he not?" ranted Alex Cameron.

"Well, I don't suppose he knew what troubles we'd have on the ship," John Sutherland conceded.

"I wonder," Alex snapped. "And I wonder if the promises he made us about the New World are as full of holes as this ship."

"Oh, surely not!" Rebecca Patterson blanched.

"If we don't get some wind, we might never find out," Alex Cameron snarled. "And here comes John Stewart with our thimbleful of water!"

"Don't be short with me," John Stewart snapped. "I just deliver the water to you. 'Tis not my fault the rations have been cut. I did not make this tub as slow as a snail."

"Aye, no point in shootin' the messenger, as it were," Archibald Chisholm soothed in his deep voice. "We don't blame you, John, for the water ration. We appreciate you bringing the bucket 'round to us."

"Humph," John Stewart grumbled. "Hard to tell, I'd say. All I hear are complaints. Someone else is welcome to the job anytime."

"Nay, nay, don't take it so. It is not you we are sore at, is it?" Archibald looked pointedly at the others.

The rest of the group gave grudging thanks to John Stewart for his efforts to bring around the water and he carried his bucket along to other settlers.

Fear festered and pustulated into suspicion and anger. There was nothing to do but wait for the wind to blow. There were some half-hearted attempts to engage the men in arm wrestling contests to help pass the time. But when one match ended in a nasty fistfight because one contestant claimed the other had cheated, and Master Spiers had to break it up and put both men in irons for a day until they cooled their tempers, the settlers went back to listless waiting.

The air was heavy, sultry, oppressive.

The first adult to die was Margaret McLean. She passed over on the second day of the calm. Margaret had been terribly seasick at the beginning of the voyage and finally succumbed to dysentery. Anne remembered when she had brought her a cup of water just a day or so out of Ullapool. Margaret had been plump and red-faced, with merry eyes and a sweet little upturned mouth. When Anne saw her just before her death, she hardly recognized her. The illness had wasted her away to little more than a skeletal husk.

Margaret's husband, William, was a stocky little fellow with rheumy eyes and a balding head. When Lily informed him that his wife of twenty years had died, he could not seem to grasp the news. He sat on the deck, the heels of his hands pressed against his temples. He shook his head over and over, not saying a word.

The funeral was held at dawn, with a crimson sun spilling over the quiet sea, as if laying a red carpet from the ship to Heaven. Captain Spiers recited the prayers, and John Sutherland, Ian, Alex Cameron, and Master Orr committed the lady's body to the crystal waters. William McLean remained mute in his grief. He did not move from the rail throughout the day, but stared out over the ocean till night shrouded everything in blackness.

Anne observed the bereaved man as she sat by the overturned longboat, gnawing listlessly on her supper of dried meat. Her eyes filled with sympathetic tears. Ian came to sit next to her.

"Is there naught we can do for him?" Anne asked.

Ian looked at poor William McLean then back at Anne. He shrugged and sighed. "I don't know. I think he has to come to terms in his own way."

Anne passed the dried meat to Ian; she had no appetite. He finished it off in a couple of quick bites.

"Ach," he said, "my throat is parched all the time."

Anne swallowed. "Mine too."

After a moment Ian said, "Do you remember the time we climbed to the top of Beinn Dearg?"

Anne frowned, thinking back. "We had gone fishing, but weren't having any luck. So we decided to follow the river up the mountain."

"Aye. We climbed right to the top. What a view!"

"It was beautiful. We sat and looked and looked for ages. Didn't get back till well after dark."

"We hadn't eaten since breakfast. Near starved."

Anne grimaced. "You and your stomach! Always hungry."

"You were hungry too, as I recall. Bleating like a lost lamb the last league to home because you were so starved."

Anne elbowed Ian in the ribs. "I did not! But we were gone a long time. My mother was not well pleased with me that night. She'd sent the boys out to search for me. Was afraid I'd fallen in the River Lael and drowned or something. My backside hurt for days."

Ian nodded, his mouth curled in a half-smile. "Not near the beating I got, though."

"My brother Will fell into the river, looking for me. He wasn't half mad about that! Came home dripping and sputtering that if I was a proper girl I'd stay home and bake bread instead of running off fishing and climbing mountains. And I said if he was a proper boy he never would have fallen in. Good thing I am a girl or he would have trounced me that day."

"And whose idea was it," Ian asked, "to go climb that mountain?"

"I don't remember," Anne said. "We probably came to the idea at the same time."

Ian snorted. He slid an arm over Anne's shoulders and as she rested her tired head on his chest, he murmured, "Another fine scrape you got me into, Anne Grant."

On the third day of the calm, in the early afternoon, the sails finally quivered and filled and the ship again lulled over the waves. Anne breathed a great sigh of relief as she felt the *Hector* roll under her feet. "Funny what a person can wish for," she thought.

After the evening meal, a young crewman in the crow's nest called out to the first mate. There was excitement in his voice. He gestured wildly toward the starboard bow.

The crew and passengers rushed to the rails and peered into the setting sun. Nothing but the endless reaches of the ocean spread before them. They looked at one another questioningly.

Captain Spiers stepped to the bow and trained his spyglass upon the western horizon. He nodded to himself, but said nothing. They all waited, watching, wondering.

And then little Christina, perched on Hugh's broad shoulders cried out, "What's that line over there? That brown line?"

The hush was broken. "What does the child see?"

"Is it land? Does she see land?"

"Captain, is it Nova Scotia?" Archibald Chisholm's bass voice boomed.

Captain Spiers turned to face the passengers. "No, not Nova Scotia. But it is land. Newfoundland. We are in sight of the New World!"

Cheers rose up from the *Hector*. Men turned and shook hands. Women hugged, crying tears of relief. Children jumped up and down and danced in circles around the deck, singing, "Land, land, Newfoundland!"

"Mister MacKay," shouted Alex Cameron to the piper, "I believe this is cause to celebrate. What about a bit of music?"

John MacKay nodded, smiling, and went to fetch his pipes. He took a moment to pass the word to the passengers below, those who were sick and those who were nursing the sick, that land was in sight. He felt it would be the best tonic of all.

John played his pipes well into the night. The Scots danced and sang, sure that their ordeal would soon be ended.

Anne stood next to the starboard rail, next to Ian. The lively music seemed to take possession of her feet. She tapped her toes in time, itching to join the dancers. Anne looked up into Ian's face, imploring him to ask her to dance.

He understood her look but shook his head sadly. "Ach, I have two left feet, lass. I'd have your shins bruised before we got once 'round the deck."

Anne tried to hide her disappointment by clapping her hands and watching Lily and John Sutherland caper across the floor. She noticed that Katherine and Hugh were dancing gaily, with Christina and Janet spinning around them like mayflies.

John Stewart strode over to Anne and bowed, flicking his blond forelock from his eyes as he straightened. "May I have the honour of this dance, madam?"

Anne beamed. "A pleasure."

She gathered her skirt in one hand and stepped out with John Stewart. She laughed as she had not laughed in weeks as her feet flew over the deck in time to the music.

When the dance ended and John Stewart escorted her back to her spot along the rail, Anne found that Ian had disappeared. Anne craned her neck, searching for him, but couldn't spot him amongst the crowd on the deck.

She started to wander aft in search of him. Then John MacKay began another frolicking tune on the pipes and John Sutherland approached Anne. He wiggled his bushy eyebrows at her and asked her to dance, and she was laughing and whirling across the deck once more.

Captain Spiers joined in the festivities for a time. Then he climbed up to the transom deck and stood between the carvings of the man and woman and surveyed the sea. The sunrise these last two mornings had been roseate and this evening's sunset was hazy. Along with the three day calm, it made him uneasy. The captain scanned the star-studded sky and breathed in the air. He watched and waited, and prayed that he waited for naught.

The captain's heart thudded heavily as he observed a dark line begin to spread across the western horizon. The darkness grew rapidly, boiling up from the sea and swallowing the stars like a gigantic maw. The breeze freshened, full of warmth and moisture.

The captain closed his eyes for a moment. Then he took a deep breath, squared his shoulders and surveyed the deck.

"Master Orr!" the captain called to his first mate.

Master Orr crossed the deck and stomped up the ladder to join the captain on the transom. The captain gestured toward the west.

Master Orr peered into the night. His eyes became round and his mouth dropped open. He glanced nervously at the captain.

"Shall I alert…?" Master Orr began.

"Let's not panic the passengers," Captain Spiers said. His tone was calm, but his face was taut. "Ask the piper to finish the celebration and have the passengers retire to the hold. Make sure none of them remains on deck. Then alert the crew. We haven't much time to secure the ship before it hits."

"Aye, Captain."

Master Orr hurried down the ladder to the piper. He whispered in John MacKay's ear.

John gazed at the first mate sidelong, disbelief written all over his face. When he saw the grim set of Master Orr's jaw, he nodded curtly. He called to the passengers, "One more song, and then I must retire for the night, and so must all of you."

"Nay, nay!" the crowd cried. "Play on, John!"

"Sorry, folks," John said cheerily, "It's late, and our dear Master Orr here tells me we may have a little wind tonight. So we need to pack up and go below."

"Nay!"

"Oh, do play on!"

"Come, come," John said. "One more song and then off to bed." And he began to play.

By the time he had finished the song and the passengers were drifting off, realizing that they could not convince him to play longer, the wind had risen considerably. Master Orr ordered his lads up onto the masts to secure the rigging. They struggled to contain the huge sheets of canvas.

There was a whistle in the wind that Anne hadn't heard before and it filled her with dread. It sounded wild, like an eagle's hunting call. She glanced about for Ian, but couldn't find him. Then she heard the wail of a frightened infant and she hurried to help Janet and Baby Jane down into the hold.

Within a quarter of an hour, the waves had whipped into froth. Rain pounded down. Anyone still on deck became drenched.

Ian was one of the last passengers to make his way down the ladder to the hold, having helped the crew secure the lines. His hair was plastered against his head. His shirt streamed water.

Anne met him at the foot of the ladder. "Did you see Christina?" she begged, her voice full of fear.

"Nay."

"Katherine cannot find her. She's nearly frantic. She thought Christina had followed her down here, but once she got the other girls in their bunk…"

"Are you sure she isn't down here somewhere? She could be in someone else's…" Ian clung to the ladder with one hand and grabbed Anne about the waist as the *Hector* rolled upon a wave, tossing them sideways.

As they righted themselves, Anne said, "We have looked and looked. Hugh has gone to search, but…"

"I'll go back up, too, and check," Ian said, turning to climb the ladder.

Anne followed him. As Ian started through the hatch he asked, "What are you doing? I'll help look for her."

"We'll both look," Anne yelled above the screaming of the wind. Her hair escaped from its pins and whipped wildly around her head. She pointed toward the stern. "I'll go aft."

Ian nodded and bent his head against the gale. He grabbed hold of a safety rope strung from the hatch to the bow and inched his way forward.

Anne planted her feet, bracing herself. Rain pelted down, soaking her in an instant. A wave crashed over the rail and washed her legs out from under her. With a yelp, she skidded across the deck and pounded against one of the doors to the crew's quarters. She rolled onto her hands and knees, sputtering and shaking icy brine from her face.

Above the roar of the waves and the whining of the wind, she thought she heard a sound. She squinted up at the transom deck. She could make out nothing in the darkness.

Anne crawled to the ladder and clung with both hands to the railing. Another frigid wave cascaded onto the deck and splashed over her. She gasped, shook the water off, and took a step upward. She pressed her body against the ladder as the ship bucked and pounded on the waves. Her fingers ached. Her knees quivered. She took another careful step. And another.

At last she was at the top of the ladder. She peered into the gloom. She could make out a small bundle lying below the carving of the woman. She inched toward it.

Anne stretched one hand out and grabbed a handful of soaked wool. She tugged, trying to pull it toward her. A tiny white face lifted from the bundle of cloth and two huge eyes stared at her. Relief flooded through Anne.

"Christina!" she shouted over the howling of the wind. "It's Anne! Come with me!"

The little girl uncurled from the carving and slid on her belly, like a seal on a slick beach rock, to face Anne.

"Good lass!" Anne cried, reaching out. "Give me your hand!"

Just then, a massive wave hit the *Hector*. The ship reeled and tipped dizzily. Anne felt herself falling backward and desperately gripped the railing with both hands. Little Christina screamed and slid along the transom deck, washed along with the brine.

"No!" Anne cried.

Christina slammed against a railing post and clung to it like a barnacle.

The ship shuddered and righted herself. Anne forced her numb fingers to let go of the railing. She scuttled on hands and knees to the edge of the transom, and grabbed Christina in her arms. The ship dropped into another trough, throwing Anne to the deck. She banged her elbows hard trying to protect Christina's little body as she fell. Anne rolled on her side and lay panting.

"I have you!" Anne yelled into the child's hair. Christina was sobbing.

Cradling Christina under one arm, Anne slithered along the wet, pitching transom deck to the ladder. She turned and slipped Christina snuggly against the ladder in front of her. They clung to the railing, their hands like claws, easing down a step at a time. Anne attempted to shield the child with her body against the worst of the rain and wind and hammering waves.

As Anne reached the bottom step, she felt strong hands grip her shoulders. She turned her soaked face, and blinking away the rain and salt spray, she recognized Captain Spiers. He did not speak. He tucked Christina securely under his arm, then placed Anne's hands, one at a time, on his waist. Anne curled her fingers around his wide leather belt and held on. Christina clung under his coat like a terrified monkey.

Crouching, fighting against the screaming wind, Captain Spiers slowly moved hand-over-hand along a rope that was strung from his cabin to mid-ship. Anne inched along behind him, clutching him as if to life itself. When the captain reached the hatch he flung it open, then passed Christina to Anne. Anne wedged the child on the ladder in front of her, and they made their way slowly to the hold below. The hatch slammed closed, shutting out some of the fury of the storm.

Anne realized that she was sobbing as hard as Christina was. She staggered between the bunks, hugging the little girl tightly as she made her way to Christina's mother. Katherine was grimly bracing Janet and Alexa in their bunk.

Katherine's face crumpled when she saw Anne, soaked and torn by the hostility of the hurricane, with her equally sorry-looking daughter in her arms. She grabbed them both in a tight embrace and wept tears of utter gratitude.

"I went to say good night to the mermaid," Christina cried, "then it got bad. I couldn't get back. I was so scared."

The *Hector* plunged into a trough that sent them all sprawling onto the floor, awash with seawater. They slowly picked themselves up and crawled to their bunks to brace themselves securely.

Shivering in her bunk, Anne fretted. Where was Ian? He would not know that she had found Christina. She dared not go back onto the deck to look for him. How long would he stay out in that terrible storm? She could feel the ship shudder as wave after wave crashed over the deck. Water spilled down through the planks onto the passengers' heads, soaking them. Ian couldn't have been swept overboard, could he? Oh, please, not that. She squeezed her eyes closed and prayed.

Presently, Anne felt a cold, sodden arm and leg press against her on the bunk. She took a deep breath and sighed, "Ian."

Anne threw her arms around his soaked, shaking shoulders. She felt his chest heave against her cheek. Ian clutched her to him.

"I could not find you. I feared …" Ian swallowed his fear, and continued. "Captain Spiers told me you had found Christina. He helped me get back to the hatch. And Hugh, too. A good man, the captain."

"Aye," Anne murmured, the salt of her tears mingling with the sea brine on her cheeks. "A good man."

"Oh, Anne. I could not bear it if anything happened to you."

Anne gripped Ian's sopping shirt in her knotted fingers. "I know. I know. I don't know what I'd do without you, Ian."

Ian kissed Anne softly on the top of her head. She turned her face up to try to see him but the hold was shrouded in a tomblike blackness. His lips travelled down her forehead, her nose, and then pressed against her mouth in a kiss that spoke of passion, relief and gratitude. They clung together, sharing what small comfort their closeness provided.

The full fury of the storm slammed into the *Hector* after midnight. The ship reeled in the churning seas, pounded and bruised by the smashing waves.

Anne had thought the storm of a few weeks ago was the worst that could possibly happen. It was mild compared to this brutal assault.

Anne clung to Ian, shivering and crying, her face buried in his chest. All around her, she heard weeping and prayers.

Anne knew that Captain Spiers would have to be manning the helm, running the ship with the wind. How was it possible that he and the crew were not swept from the deck?

The *Hector* moaned as wave after monstrous wave threatened to bury her. Again and again, the sea tried to fold the *Hector* within its watery arms. It seemed it would not be denied this small prize. And yet, somehow, the ship fought her way to the top of every crushing wave. As she plunged into deep troughs, she lifted her stubborn bow and struggled her way upward, only to have the storm batter her down once more.

Dawn came, though the passengers had no way of knowing in the dark hold. The hurricane raged on through the morning and afternoon. There was no food or water during all that time. No one dared move from where they were wedged. And who would keep anything in their stomachs?

As the hours of merciless chaos wore on, the passengers – especially the children, the sick and the infirm – fell into an exhausted stupor. A kind of hopeless resignation descended over them all. They prepared themselves for what seemed inevitable.

Anne realized that she must have actually slipped into a fretful doze. She came to as Ian shifted his weight beside her. She straightened slightly and opened her eyes. It took a moment for her to notice that she didn't have to brace herself so strenuously to stay in the bunk.

Ian gave her shoulders a little squeeze. He whispered, "I think the storm is passing."

Anne sighed. Did she dare hope?

The hold remained as dark as pitch. How long had they been there? It was impossible to tell.

"Too rough yet to go above," Ian said in Anne's ear.

Anne nodded. The ship tossed and pounded on the waves, but the mad fury of the storm had lessened.

Anne's entire body ached as if she had been beaten. Her frantic search for Christina and the hours of rigid tension left her so sore she could hardly move. Her elbows were throbbing. Her skin felt raw in her sodden clothing.

"Try to sleep if you can, lass," Ian suggested. He settled her against him and she closed her eyes. Exhaustion washed over her.

The hurricane moved off the following morning, thirty-two hours after Captain Spiers had spied the dark cloud in the western sky. The sea swell heaved the *Hector* over waves the height of crags, but the wind had abated. Passengers slowly eased their battered bodies from the hold to survey the damage.

It had been considerable. Evidence of hasty repairs during the storm showed the extent of damage the hurricane had caused. A tattered sail, folded and stowed on the deck, waited to be sewn. Ropes that had snapped in the violence of the wind lay coiled on the deck. Crewmen were rushing to make the ship fully seaworthy again. Anne marveled that the *Hector*, with her leaks and rotten planks, had held together. She dropped to her knees and gave a prayer of thanks.

The settlers were just taking in the damage that had been done when Archibald Chisholm came above and sadly announced that four children had died during the storm. Little Walter Murray and Colin McKay, both toddlers, had succumbed to the smallpox while the hurricane raged. Cousins, Ken and Katie MacKenzie, who had been lively, freckle-faced youths, were also dead. Captain Spiers grimly held a funeral service for all four children.

The joy and celebration of two nights ago was drowned in the storm and buried at sea with the children.

Chapter 10

THERE WAS NO CHATTER of conversation on board. Passengers sat in silent, disconsolate groups. Hope had been torn from them bit by bit throughout this voyage till at last they were left as battered as the ship itself.

Archibald Chisholm approached Anne, Ian, Hugh, Katherine, and the girls on the evening after the storm. His face was deeply lined.

He took a deep breath and said, "Master Orr has told me that the hurricane has blown us off course."

"Aye, well, that's no surprise," Hugh said.

Archibald nodded. "Master Orr informs me that it will likely take a fortnight to regain the distance."

"A fortnight!" Hugh exclaimed. "That can't be right."

"I am afraid that the captain has plotted our position most carefully and thinks it will take us two weeks to come in sight of Newfoundland again."

The group stood in a horrified astonishment.

Archibald squared his shoulders and said quietly, "And it seems our rations are becoming very… uh… meagre. We shall have to go on half rations or we may not have food to last out the voyage."

Katherine gathered her girls close to her. "Surely the children's rations…"

Archibald Chisholm shook his head sadly.

Katherine gasped. Hugh put a hand on his wife's shoulder and said, "We will share our rations with them, Katherine. Our girls will not go hungry."

Katherine gazed up into Hugh's face and nodded.

Archibald moved along the deck to continue spreading the news. Hugh said, "I have the oatcakes, you know. The ones that people were going to throw overboard."

"Did they not get ruined in the storm, Hugh?" Katherine asked.

"Nay, I don't think so. I have them carefully put away. I'll check on them now, and if they are not full of sea water, I'll take them straight away to the captain."

As Hugh strode off to retrieve his cache of moldy oatcakes, Ian said, "Many scoffed at him, calling him a miserly old woman. We may praise the Lord, and our good Hugh, for those oatcakes yet."

The sun beat down upon them the following afternoon, making the settlers all seek patches of shade on the parched deck. Anne was in her lightest cotton smock, fanning herself with a tattered handkerchief. Ian sprawled next to her, his hat over his eyes. John Stewart plunked himself down next to Anne's other side.

"Fierce hot," he commented.

Anne nodded and dabbed beads of sweat from her forehead and upper lip. She noticed John's eyes on her. She felt rather indecently clothed under his scrutiny.

"I don't reckon it ever got this hot in Greenock," John allowed. "Always a breeze off the water. A lovely place, Greenock."

"Is it?" Anne asked, out of politeness rather than curiosity.

"Aye, sure. A grand place." And John went on at length to tell Anne all about the town's virtues.

Anne squirmed on her seat of canvas sacks, and glanced at Ian. Ian might have been asleep, but for the occasional soft derisive snort that escaped from under the hat at key moments during John's oration.

John continued, "I've lived there since I was a lad. My da was a fisherman. Took me out in his boat as soon as I could walk."

Ian heaved himself to his feet and mumbled something about needing to see Hugh. He tromped aft. Anne watched him go. John said, "A quiet sort of chap, isn't he?" and then continued his tale about his exploits as a young man growing up in the coastal town.

A couple of days later, when Anne settled next to the MacLeods for their half-ration supper, she noticed that Christina wasn't eating. The little girl took a sip of water, but didn't touch her salt meat or piece of oatcake.

"It's all right to eat what you have," Anne whispered to her. "There will be food enough to see us through. Don't worry about what Mister Chisholm said."

Christina looked up at Anne. Her eyes were glassy and her cheeks were flushed. "I'm not hungry," she whimpered.

Anne's stomach clenched. She set her own food down and reached out to touch Christina's forehead. It was hot.

"Katherine," Anne croaked, her throat suddenly very dry.

Katherine looked up from feeding little Alexa. Her face puckered with worry when she saw the expression in Anne's eyes.

"I… I don't think Christina is feeling well."

Katherine was beside her eldest child in an instant. "Dear merciful God," she murmured. Then she called to her husband, who was talking with Alexander.

"Hugh!"

Hugh glanced over. Seeing the panic on Katherine's face, he left his brother and came to her.

Katherine whispered, "Christina is sick. She has a fever."

"What should we do?" Hugh asked.

"I'll take her below. You tell Captain Spiers and then look after the other two girls." Katherine scooped Christina up in her arms and hurried to the hold, her cheeks wet with tears.

Anne said, "I'll watch the girls while you speak to the captain, Hugh. Then I'll go help Katherine."

Hugh nodded his thanks. He hurried off.

Anne gave the rest of her meal to little Janet. She had no more appetite.

When Hugh returned, Anne rushed to the hold. Captain Spiers was examining Christina. The child lay like her rag doll upon the bunk.

"I do not think she has the smallpox," Captain Spiers stated after his examination. "Although it may be too soon to tell."

Katherine folded her hands as if in silent prayer.

"Perhaps the fright and soaking she got in the storm has brought this on." The captain shook his head. "Cover her well. I will send down a tisane that may help."

The captain left. Katherine held little Christina's limp hand and shed silent tears. Anne stood next to her, not knowing what to say or do.

A deckhand appeared later with a cup of warm liquid. "The cap'n sent this," he said.

Anne took the cup and the lad hurried away. She held it out to Katherine.

Katherine took a steadying breath. She took the cup. "Would you," she whispered, "hold her head up for me?"

Anne slid onto the edge of the bunk by Christina's head. She eased the child's shoulders forward, allowing her tiny weight to lean against her chest.

Katherine carefully tipped the tea to Christina's lips. When the child did not respond, Katherine coaxed, "Come on, lass. This is from the captain. You need to drink it. Just a sip. That's it."

Anne and Katherine managed to get most of the liquid into the child before she fell into a feverish slumber. They covered her with blankets and cloaks.

"I'll watch her if you want to check on Janet and Alexa," Anne offered.

Katherine shook her head. "This is where I need to be."

Anne nodded.

Katherine reached out a hand and patted Anne on the shoulder. "Thank you for being here to help."

Anne said, "You know I'll do what I can."

Ian came below later to check on them.

"Hugh and the girls are fine," he told Katherine. "Elspie is helping."

"Thank you," Katherine said wearily.

"Why don't you get a little sleep?" Anne asked Katherine. "I'll stay up and watch."

Ian said, "You do look tired, Katherine. You can use our bunk if you like. I am sleeping on deck tonight."

Katherine regarded her daughter. Christina's small face was beaded with sweat; her skin appeared translucent. Katherine said, "I should stay here."

Ian shrugged and headed up the ladder.

"I really don't mind sitting with her," Anne said.

"I know. I know. But I'm afraid... I'm afraid if I don't watch her... I need to be with her... I can't explain."

Anne searched her friend's anguished face. The deep love and heart-wrenching worry were right on the surface. Of course Katherine could not leave her child's side. What if Death crept up in the night and touched Christina while Katherine was not on guard? She would never forgive herself for not being here, for not doing all that she could to fight against him, to beat him back.

"All right. I'm going to bed. In the morning, I will take a watch, if you like. Call me if you need me." Anne crawled into her bunk and slipped into a fitful sleep.

When she woke in the morning, she found Katherine as she had left her, sitting by Christina's bunk, holding her small, frail fingers.

Anne whispered, "Any change?"

Katherine blinked red-rimmed, bleary eyes. "Nay."

Anne smoothed the auburn tendrils of damp hair from Christina's brow. The child's forehead was still hot. Anne sat on the edge of the bunk across the narrow aisle.

Captain Spiers arrived to check on Christina. He only said, "I'll send down another tisane."

Anne stood. "I'll go get our breakfasts and bring them down."

"I'm not hungry," Katherine murmured.

"Hungry or no," Anne said in a Lily Sutherland voice, "you need to eat and keep your strength up. For Christina."

Anne went off in search of food. When she returned, Katherine had the tisane. They sat Christina up between them and dribbled some of it into her mouth.

Then they ate their pitiful breakfast.

Katherine's face held more life once she had eaten. "I guess I did need that," she said.

"Oh, aye," Anne answered. "You also need a bit of sleep. Your eyes look like black pits."

Katherine looked down at her daughter's face.

"I will let you know if there is any change at all. Why don't we try to get a wee bit more tisane in her, and then you have a nap?"

Katherine gave a grudging nod.

Anne kept vigil beside the child during the morning. When Katherine woke, Anne went up on deck for a breath of fresh air and her midday meal. She joined Hugh, Alexander, Elspie and all the children.

"Christina is the same," she reported. "No change."

Lily approached Anne as she finished her dry and tasteless oatcake. Lily said, "I was busy with Janet Fraser last night, or I would have been down to help you and Katherine."

"Baby Jane isn't sick, is she?" Anne asked anxiously.

"Colic. She's fine now. I'll go help Katherine this afternoon. You rest. Maybe you can help tonight?"

Anne nodded, relieved to have Lily with Katherine.

Anne found where Ian had slept the night before, in the lee of the longboat. She curled up on the pile of canvas and cloaks and closed her eyes.

She felt Ian sit down next to her. He put his hand on her shoulder, and with that bit of comfort, she drifted into sleep.

Anne made her way to the musty hold. The air was as fetid as ever. She braced herself against the putrid smells and took her place next to Christina's bunk. The little girl lay still and pale under the covers.

Katherine was bathing her forehead with a damp rag and softly humming a hymn. She looked up as Anne approached.

"Is she no better?" Anne asked.

Katherine shook her head. "The fever eats at her. She has no strength. She does not even whimper in her sleep now."

Katherine had aged ten years. Deep lines creased her face. Her eyes were dull and sunken. Her cheeks, which had been round and soft at the beginning of the voyage, were sunken so the bones jutted out sharply.

"Have you eaten?" Anne queried.

Katherine nodded. "Lily brought me a bite. And she sat with Christina for a while this afternoon. But I couldn't sleep."

"Why don't you go for a wee walk up on deck? Get some fresh air. Janet and Alexa would be glad to see you, too."

"All right. Aye. A short walk. I'll take up the bucket to empty. I will not be long."

Anne patted Katherine's hand. It felt clammy. "Take a cloak," she suggested.

Katherine gave Anne a wan smile and slipped off for a brief break.

Anne touched little Christina's forehead. It was still raging hot.

Anne whispered to the child about the New World, about the trees that grew right to the water's edge, the rivers full of fish, the forests full of animals. She talked of how they would be free to talk as they wished, think as they wished, dress as they wished. After a bit, Anne thought she might be describing Heaven. Was Nova Scotia really a paradise on Earth or was that too good to be true?

Katherine returned. The brisk evening air had put a little colour in her face. She thanked Anne.

"Please, Katherine, get some sleep. I will stay."

Katherine shook her head. "There is no sleep for me. I am that worried."

"Then I'll sit up with you. Keep you company."

"Aye. All right. That would be nice."

They spoke very little through the night. The dark hours dragged as the ship creaked and sighed over the waves.

Christina began to thrash and flail shortly before dawn. Anne and Katherine restrained her so she wouldn't fling herself from the bunk. She was eerily silent through her convulsions.

Her lids fluttered open once, but her eyes rolled up into her head and she saw nothing.

At last, the fit ended and Christina lay limp and spent on the bunk. Anne hurried to the captain's cabin. She knocked on the door, then waited, hopping from one bare foot to the other, trying to warm herself in the predawn chill. She knocked again, harder this time. The cabin door flew open. The captain stood before her in shirt and breeches, his feet and head bare.

"I... Excuse me for waking you, sir. But the child, Christina, has had a fit. Could you come?"

"At once. Let me get my bag."

Anne rushed back to the hold. The captain was only moments behind her.

Katherine sat hugging herself, rocking back and forth. Her teeth were chattering.

Anne feared that Christina was not breathing as she approached the bunk.

Katherine did not even look up when the captain approached. Captain Spiers took Katherine by the shoulders and gently but firmly moved her to the end of the bunk. Then he sat by Christina's side and examined her closely.

"How long did the seizure last?" he asked.

Anne thought. It seemed to last forever! "It was only a few minutes, I suppose. It seemed a long time."

The captain nodded. "Has she been coughing?"

"Nay."

"It is the fever that gave her the fit." He thought for a long moment. "Let us get her cooled down."

"But, Captain!" Katherine exclaimed, shaken from her stupor. "Does she not have to sweat out the disease?"

"If she has not done so by now, she is not likely to. And she cannot bear the fever much longer."

Captain Spiers threw the covers off the sick child and began to remove her clothing.

Katherine raised a hand to protest. Then looking at Christina's ravaged face, she shuddered. Silently, she helped to undo the child's frock.

Once the girl was stripped down to her petticoat, Captain Spiers took the damp rag and sponged her head, arms and legs. The moisture evaporated off Christina's hot skin in an instant. He went over her frail body again and again with the cloth.

Eventually, he passed the rag to Anne, saying, "Keep doing this. I am going to make her a medicine. I will not be long."

The captain hurried above deck and returned with a warm, acrid-smelling drink. Anne tilted Christina's head while he carefully dribbled it into her mouth. Some of it escaped down her chin, but she swallowed a good measure of the concoction.

"Continue to cool her with the damp cloth," the captain instructed. "Let me know if there's a change."

"Aye," Anne murmured.

Captain Spiers turned to speak to Katherine. She was slumped against the foot of the bunk, her eyes closed.

At first, Anne thought her friend had slipped into an exhausted sleep. When the captain swore under his breath, Anne sat up and peered through the gloom. Her mouth fell open, horrified. Katherine's skin shimmered with sweat. Her face was pallid.

Captain Spiers regained his composure. "You will have to care for the child," he stated. "Where shall I put Mistress MacLeod? I need to move her away from this bunk."

"My bunk," Anne choked through tears. "You may put her in my bunk, over there." She pointed.

Captain Spiers nodded. He gently picked Katherine up in his arms and carried her to Anne's bunk. He lay her down and covered her with blankets.

"I will inform her husband," he said grimly. The captain strode to the ladder.

"Dear God in Heaven," Anne prayed, "Not Katherine and little Christina. Please."

Lily Sutherland bustled into the hold a short time later, Hugh trailing after her. When Hugh saw Katherine, he snatched off his hat. He gripped it tightly in both hands, crushing the brim. His lips trembled.

Lily took a deep steadying breath, then sat on the bunk next to Katherine. She picked up the young woman's hand and said, "Katherine."

Katherine's eyes fluttered open. It took a moment for her to focus in the gloom. Katherine looked from Lily to Hugh. "I'm sorry," she whispered.

"Lass, you have naught to be sorry for," Lily said. "You are worn out from caring for your wee one. You get some rest and you will be right as rain."

Katherine said, "Lily, you do not need to put sugar on it. I know I am sick. Just see that my girls are looked after."

Lily sighed. "Have you ever had the cowpox, Katherine?"

"Nay."

"I need to get some things. I will be right back."

Lily slipped away. Hugh gazed down at his wife, his face contorted in a grimace of worry.

Katherine held his eyes for a long moment. "Look after our girls, Hugh. No matter what."

"I will," he murmured. "You know I will."

Katherine nodded and closed her eyes.

Lily returned. "Perhaps you should get back to the children," she suggested to Hugh.

Hugh gave a curt nod and strode away.

Anne swallowed the lump that had risen in her throat and continued to bathe little Christina. "Don't you worry, Katherine," she whispered, "I'll care of Christina as if she were my own."

During the mid-morning, Christina's fever broke. Anne covered her over with a light blanket. The child murmured in her sleep, sighed, and lay peacefully.

Anne sat with Christina till Rebecca Patterson came below. Rebecca folded her willowy form onto a nearby bunk and said, "I'll stay with her for a bit. Get some air and a bite to eat."

Anne nodded her thanks. She stopped to ask Lily how Katherine was. The older woman shook her head and said, "Time will tell."

Anne leaned over the bunk and said, "Katherine, Christina's fever has broken."

Katherine's eyelids flickered, but she made no reply.

Anne found the captain in his cabin. She reported on Katherine and Christina, then went out on the deck.

Anne welcomed the cool sea air and bright sunlight. She stood at the starboard rail for a time, gazing off where the pale blue of the sky met the sapphire blue of the sea. Ian found her there.

"How is she?"

"Christina's fever broke. Katherine is very poorly."

"And how are you?"

"Oh, Ian, I am heartsick. So much pain. So much grief. How much more can we bear?" Anne threw her hands over her face and great sobs welled up.

Ian wrapped his arms around her and held her tightly. He said nothing. He let her cry till the sobbing subsided.

"I have your noon meal. Will you sit and eat with me before you return to the wee one?" he asked.

Anne nodded and followed Ian to the space on the deck where he had been sleeping. She sat upon the pile of canvas and blankets and chewed and swallowed the food without really tasting any of it.

"Elspie is grand with Janet and Alexa," Ian said. "And her three lads get along well with the girls."

"That's good of Elspie."

"Poor Hugh is at a loss. He tries, but with both Christina and Katherine sick…. Well, he has a great deal on his mind."

"Aye. I'll go tell him that Christina seems a bit better before I go below." Anne touched Ian's cheek. "Thank you."

Ian grinned at her lopsidedly.

Anne found Hugh at the bow, talking with John Sutherland and Archibald Chisholm. She gave Hugh what news she could. She filled a cup with water, then returned to the hold.

Rebecca reported, "She didn't wake."

"Thank you, Rebecca."

"I'll be back again later."

Anne slid her arm behind Christina's shoulders to sit her up and held the cup of water to her lips. "Come on, lass. Try to drink. There's a good girl."

When the liquid touched her lips, Christina moved her face away, but as Anne persisted, she finally took a swallow. Anne eased her back onto the bunk.

The fever returned in the late afternoon, but not so high as before. Anne moistened the child's skin through the evening and into the night. In the early morning, the fever again broke.

Anne sat, half dozing, her head propped on her hand. A tiny noise brought her eyes open.

Christina was looking at her. Anne straightened and smiled. "There's my lass."

Christina blinked and rolled her head back and forth. She swallowed loudly and croaked, "Thirsty."

Anne grabbed the cup of water and helped Christina sit up to drink. The child could only manage a small sip. Christina slumped back on the bunk.

"Are you warm enough?" Anne asked.

Christina frowned. She gave her head a slight nod.

"Good. I'll stay here with you. Let me know if you need anything."

The frown smoothed from the child's forehead and she slept. Anne sighed. Maybe, just maybe, they were through the worst.

Chapter 11

Anne felt a warm hand on her shoulder. She blinked her gritty eyes open to see Ian looking down at her. She was slumped at the foot of Christina's bunk, her legs dangling over the edge. Anne sat up slowly and rubbed her shins to bring the blood to her numb limbs.

Ian held out a cup of steaming liquid.

Anne took it and inhaled deeply. "Where did you get…?"

"The captain sent it down."

"For Christina?"

"No, lass, for you. He thought you were that tired, and needed it."

Anne breathed in the wonderful tea aroma, then sipped it slowly, savouring. She glanced over to their bunk. Rebecca Patterson sat with Katherine.

"She is no better?" Anne asked.

Ian shook his head.

Anne had trouble swallowing the last of her tea. She passed the cup back to Ian with a quiet, "Thank you." Then she turned to little Christina and lay a hand on her forehead. The child's temperature seemed fine.

"At least she is over the fever," Anne murmured.

"Aye. Now, would you like a bit of breakfast? I will stay here with the wee one so you can get some air."

"Nay, if you will just bring something down to me, please, I think I'll stay here. In case she wakes."

Ian paused to bend and kiss Anne on the cheek. Then he turned and left.

In the quiet of the hold, Anne noticed four other women keeping their silent vigil over a sick companion or loved one.

She sighed and tugged the blanket about Christina's small shoulders.

She stepped over to gaze down upon Katherine. Her friend lay motionless on the bunk, her mahogany hair matted against her sweat-soaked face.

Rebecca whispered, "She thrashed a bit in the night, but since dawn, she has not so much as twitched. I tried to get her to take some water, but couldn't get her to swallow a drop."

"Let us try together," Anne suggested.

With Anne holding her shoulders and Rebecca tilting the cup, they managed to wet Katherine's lips, but she could not drink.

Anne bit her lip as she eased her friend back onto the bunk. Rebecca's eyes met hers and she shook her head.

Lily arrived then to relieve Rebecca. She regarded Anne's pinched face and demanded, "Who is sitting with Christina this morning so you can rest, Anne?"

"I... I don't mind...."

"If you get too tired, you'll be the next one we have to nurse. Now, go up on deck and have a proper sleep. Rebecca, please ask Marion to come down. She can be with the child for a while." When she saw that Anne hesitated, Lily commanded, "Go!"

Anne stumbled up the ladder. Lily was right, Anne knew, as tears flooded her vision. She collapsed on canvas sacking and fell into a troubled sleep.

The few hours of sleep did refresh her a little, and when she returned to Christina in the afternoon, the sight of the little girl awake and alert made her heart warm.

"Well, lass, you are awake," Anne greeted her.

"Aye," Christina croaked.

Marion said, "She's had a bit of water, but naught yet to eat."

"Do you feel hungry?" Anne asked hopefully.

Christina shook her head.

"Well, perhaps by suppertime."

Marion eased away and Anne sat by the bunk on an overturned bucket. She held the girl's hand.

"Are Mama and Papa angry with me?" Christina whispered.

Anne's eyes opened wide. "Why would you think that, lass?"

"I should never have gone to the mermaid that night. The night of the storm. And then I got sick and made all this trouble...."

"Oh, Christina, nay." Anne leaned forward and gave her a hug. "Your mama and papa are not angry. They are just worried. Now that you are feeling better, they are right glad."

"Then where is Mama?" the child wailed.

Anne sat back and looked at Christina sadly. At last she explained, "She's feeling poorly, lass, and needs to rest herself right now. So she asked me to sit with you. Would that be all right for now?"

Christina's eyes were dull but she nodded. Anne hoped she hadn't upset the child. Christina would need all the spirit she could muster to recover.

Anne coaxed some oatcake softened in water into her charge at suppertime. She made sure Christina had the best portion of food that she could find. Then she watched as sleep washed over the little girl.

Anne's next few days were filled with caring for Christina. Christina ate and drank small portions and slowly began to gain strength.

During that time, Katherine's fever ravaged her body; she was rarely conscious.

After a few days, Lily suggested that the little girl be brought up on deck. The fresh air and activity might brighten her up. Hugh came below to carry her up the ladder.

As they made their way past Katherine, Christina twisted in Hugh's arms, pointing at the prone figure on the bunk. She cried out, "Mama! Mama! That's my mama!"

Hugh's lips pressed together. He held his tiny daughter tightly as he hurried up the ladder. Christina was sobbing as he set her gently on a bed of cloaks near the bow. "Mama, Mama!" she wailed. Hugh held her in his arms and rocked her to and fro.

Elspie rushed over. Hugh's face was grief-stricken as he murmured, "She saw Katherine as I brought her up."

Elspie sighed and nodded. She knelt by the terrified girl and stroked her red curls and whispered in her ear as Hugh continued to rock her in his arms. Eventually, her sobs subsided and Christina fell into an exhausted sleep.

"Thank you," Hugh said earnestly to his sister-in-law.

Elspie patted his shoulder. "You are welcome, Hugh. I'll do whatever I can."

He nodded. "I know. You are a good woman."

Sorrow marked the day. Later that morning, a Ross youth succumbed to smallpox. Before his funeral prayers were finished, a second child, a six-year-old girl of the Munroe family, passed away. A second funeral was performed before noon.

The following day, Anne did her best to amuse Christina, trying to distract her from worrying over her mother. Anne felt like a fly about a donkey's ears – buzzing around, but accomplishing little except to irritate the girl. Christina ignored her for the most part, drawing within herself.

It was Elspie and her boys, and Janet and Alexa, who finally brought Christina out of her shell. The children frolicked nearby and little by little Christina was drawn into their games. Elspie was always close by to scold and cuddle and laugh, providing Christina the mothering she craved.

Anne realized Christina did not need her. She felt hurt at first, then shook off the resentment as being silly and selfish, and took herself where she was needed. She descended to the hold and settled next to Katherine's bedside.

She was sitting in the dank hold when she heard the lookout shout, "Newfoundland!" This time, there was no jubilation aboard the *Hector*. Superstitious fear swept over the Scots. There were many anxious glances at the western sky and earnest, nervous prayers.

The pox appeared over Katherine's face and limbs that evening. Anne had been quite sure that Katherine had smallpox, but it repulsed her to actually see the welts contort and redden Katherine's pale skin.

As the *Hector* scudded past the Avalon Peninsula of Newfoundland, Lily came below to relieve Anne.

"Is there any hope?" Anne asked plaintively.

Lily shook her head but said, "Where there's life, there is always hope."

"I feel so helpless. Why is there naught we can do for her? She is a good woman. She does not deserve this."

Lily grimaced. "Most do not, lass."

"How do you keep going, Lily? You have nursed so many this voyage and there have been... how many lost? Sixteen? Seventeen?"

"Why do you think I'm such a cranky old goat?" Lily said, one corner of her lips lifting. "You need a bit of flint in your heart or you go mad from the grief."

Anne gave a weary smile. She hugged the dour matron and said softly, "I think it's all an act, Lily. I think you are the dearest, most generous soul on this ship."

Lily blinked rapidly several times and turned her head as if to check on Katherine's blankets. "Off with you, now, to get some food and sleep. I'll expect you back here in a few hours to watch again, mind."

Anne kissed Lily's cheek as she rose to go above.

She woke to angry words.

"You can't be serious!"

"Well, it is your choice, Mr. Cameron. You can eat this or go hungry. It is all the same to me." John Sutherland was speaking in a low, controlled voice.

"I do not believe there is naught left but this foul trash!" Alex Cameron yelled.

"Are you calling me a liar, then?" John Sutherland asked, menace creeping into his mild voice.

"I'm saying the captain is keeping the best of the supplies for himself and his pompous mate and he's letting us eat this garbage."

"There is no more food!" John's voice had risen to a shout. Passengers froze, eyes captured by this hot exchange. "You fool, we have been at sea far longer than was planned for. The storm blew us halfway back to Scotland! These oatcakes that Hugh saved are all that's left!"

A heavy silence hung over the ship.

Alex Cameron blanched, then colour rose in his face, flushing his cheeks and neck a vivid red. His eyes narrowed and he bent his head to glare into John's face. "We'll see about this. You are such grand friends with Hugh MacLeod. Maybe he knows where the decent food is and is eating well while you are handing out this slop to the rest of us."

John's nostrils flared. His fists clenched. "How dare you accuse –"

"What is all this?" a voice barked. Alex Cameron spun around to find the captain striding up to them.

"Mister Sutherland," Alex spat, "is trying to tell me that there are no provisions left but these moldy oatcakes, Captain."

Captain Spiers stood with his back ramrod straight, his hands clasped behind his back. His face darkened into a scowl.

Alex continued. "There must still be decent foodstuffs aboard, Captain, and I demand to have my share of them. I paid my fare, and I deserve my allotment of daily rations. It is bad enough that we have been cut down to half the share we were promised. And now this!"

John Sutherland glared at Alex Cameron from under his bushy brows. "You get what the rest of us get."

"And how do I know that there is not a nice little cache of salt meat tucked away for you and your friends?" Alex sneered.

"So," the captain stated, "Mister Cameron, you feel there is food aplenty hidden away on this ship?"

Alex's eyes shifted from John Sutherland to the captain. He lifted his chin and said, "There must be more than these miserable foul things." He gestured to the oatcakes that John held.

"Very well, Mister Cameron. Since you are so convinced, we will allow Mister Sutherland to continue to distribute oatcakes to those who are grateful to have such as this to eat. And you will come below with me. You will search the hold for other provisions and you may partake of any that you find there."

Alex Cameron shuffled his feet. He regarded the firm set of the captain's jaw. He glanced about at his fellow passengers. Those who would meet his eyes held hard, contemptuous stares.

John nodded to the captain and stepped away, passing out the ration of oatcakes. No one else refused the spoiled food.

Alex Cameron swallowed loudly, causing his Adam's apple to bobble. "Follow me," the captain commanded. He turned on his heel, headed for the cargo deck.

Alex trailed after him saying, "Uh, perhaps, Captain, I was a bit hasty...."

Without looking over his shoulder, the captain snapped, "Before you think again to call any man on my ship a liar, Mister Cameron, you had best know the facts. And for your supper tonight you will eat only those fine provisions that you find hidden away."

Alex Cameron had a long and hungry night.

Chapter 12

Rebecca Patterson offered to watch Katherine through the night so both Lily and Anne could get a decent sleep. Anne settled next to Ian on their pile of canvas, but she could not close her eyes. Every time she did, Katherine's ravaged face floated before her. At last she sat up.

Ian pushed himself up on an elbow and regarded her, chin in hand. At last he whispered, "Cannot sleep?"

Anne murmured, "Nay."

Ian sat up and put his arm around Anne's waist, drawing her near him. Anne let her head drop to his shoulder. The creak of the ropes and the hiss of the waves filled their silence. Then Anne sighed, "What will Hugh do? How will he manage with three little girls, all alone?"

Ian did not answer. There seemed to be none.

"She is a dear woman. Full of kindness. And spirit. A good friend." Anne brushed her cheek with the back of her hand. "She should not die. Oh, Ian, it's not right that she should die."

Ian stroked her hair, and kissed the top of her head. He let her cry without interrupting her sorrow with words.

When Anne's tears were spent, Ian took both of her hands in his. He peered at her in the summer night, their only light the reflection of the stars on the smooth waves.

"Anne," he whispered.

Her eyes met his.

"Anne," he repeated. He sighed. "I cannot bear the thought that we could be separated. Ever. We have been through so much. I know now that I need you with me. I know you came with me to escape marriage to MacDonald. I know I am naught to you but a friend. But I would like… Oh Anne… If you would have me as your husband.…"

His words flooded Anne with joy and overwhelming peace, like a hot drink on a January day. The desire to laugh, to cry, to sing, to shout, bubbled up into her heart.

Courage left Ian. His gaze dropped to the deck. He loosed his hold on her fingers, and began to turn from her.

"Ian," she whispered urgently. She reached out and placed her palm on his warm cheek. He slowly brought his eyes back to meet hers.

Anne bit her trembling lip, then said, softly but clearly, "I would be so honoured to have you as my husband. You are the most dear, caring man.... How could I go on without you?"

Ian gaped at her a moment, then grabbed her in a bear hug that crushed the air from her. She gasped and threw her arms around his neck. He eased his grip just enough to bring his head down so he could kiss her, warmly, passionately, on the mouth. When his lips touched hers, it was sweet – as sweet as the first crisp, juicy apple in autumn.

Then he whispered in her ear, "I love you, Anne Grant."

"I love you, Ian. Aye, I love you, too."

"I'll speak with the captain," Ian whispered into her hair. "I will see if he will marry us before we leave the ship."

Anne sighed. "Do you not think he'll be angry? We lied about being husband and wife to get aboard...."

Ian thought a moment. "Let me speak with him," was all he said.

They lay with their arms wrapped about one another. The gentle rocking of the *Hector* eventually soothed them into sleep.

Breakfast consisted of the pitiful moldy oatcakes. Ian used his knife to cut away the worst of the spoiled edges for Anne. They tasted foul, and washed down with stale water, they did little to satisfy the appetite.

The sun was just beginning to lift the morning fog when there was a great splash near the ship. The settlers cried out in surprise. Many rushed to the starboard rail and peered into the misty morning. Just when they were starting to think they had imagined the noise, another great splash rippled the wispy fog.

"What was that?" Rebecca Patterson squeaked.

A sound like rushing air came out of the mists and then an enormous dark shape loomed up next to the *Hector*. Passengers gasped and shuffled back from the rail.

"It's a sea monster!" a woman screamed.

The settlers began to yell and mill about in panic. The captain strode into their midst and barked, "Silence! Stand fast!" Everyone froze.

The shape in the water raised its back and then lifted its magnificent T-shaped tail. The tail must have been fifteen feet across, white with an edging of black. It slipped noiselessly below the surface. The passengers stood in awe, their mouths agape.

"That creature is a whale," the captain announced. "A humpback whale. They feed in these waters. They are quite harmless to ships."

The settlers huddled uneasily, staring at the sea.

About thirty feet from the bow, the whale erupted from the water and crashed upon the waves. The wake of its splash rocked the *Hector*. A few of the settlers scuttled below, making the sign of the cross as they went; most stood in silent fascination, transfixed by the magnificence of the creature.

It dove again, then several moments later, resurfaced, spouting a fountain of moist air through its blowhole. The whale swam atop the waves for a time and then crashed its huge white flipper on the surface, drumming the sea. Eventually, it rolled and dove, displaying its astonishing tail once more.

It was the most majestic thing Anne had ever seen. Such power and grace. It quite took her breath away. She glanced up into Ian's face and saw her awed amazement mirrored in his eyes.

The humpback had been feeding just off the coast of Cape Breton Island, the northern tip of Nova Scotia. They sighted the island as the morning fog lifted.

Anne braced her resolve and went below. Lily was there already. Katherine lay limp, her breath rasping. The pox marred her face so that she was hardly recognizable.

Anne swallowed loudly twice, thrice, then made for a bucket and retched. She knelt, shivering over the bucket for a time, till her head stopped reeling. At last, she got unsteadily to her feet. She stood with one hand on a bunk, then bent and picked up the bucket. Wordlessly she carried it up on deck, emptied it, and scrubbed it out.

John Stewart approached her. "Ah, Anne. A word with you?"

"Oh, John, not now."

He frowned.

Anne sighed. "I am busy, with Katherine, you know. And besides, John…"

"I see," he cut her off. He skulked across the deck toward some men at the bow.

Anne shook her head and returned to Katherine's bedside.

Lily glanced up at her, but said not a word. She simply took Anne's cold hand in her own for a moment, giving it a squeeze.

They sponged Katherine's hot forehead and wet her dry, chapped lips throughout the day. They spoke little.

Rebecca came to relieve them at sunset. Anne and Lily trudged wearily to the deck. The sun blazed to a crimson and violet end over a silver sea.

Anne leaned on the rail and watched the day die.

Ian came to her as the last tendrils of light streaked the western horizon. He waited till Anne turned her face toward him.

"I talked with Captain Spiers," he said, his tone even.

Anne waited. There could be no joy, she feared. The master of the ship would be very angry with them. He probably refused Ian's request. He may even plan to punish them.

Ian said softly, "Did you mean what you said last night?"

Anne's backbone straightened. "Of course I did! How could you doubt…?"

"Well," Ian continued in a quiet voice, "if you have a mind to, Captain Spiers would be pleased to see us in his cabin."

"Now?"

"Aye." Ian did not move. He waited for her.

Anne was so weighed down with the heavy grief of her day, it took a long moment to shake free of it. She looked out at the darkening sky, and spied the first star as it pricked the eastern heavens with a pinpoint of light. She took a deep breath and reached out to touch Ian's cheek.

"Let us not keep the good captain waiting any longer, then," she said at last.

Ian's face lit in a dazzling smile. He took her hand and they walked together to the stern. Ian knocked lightly on the captain's door, and when bade enter, he led Anne within.

Lily and John Sutherland were seated at the captain's table. Anne looked at them questioningly.

"We need two witnesses," Ian explained. "I thought it would be all right...."

"We shall not tell a soul," Lily said in her matter-of-fact way.

Anne nodded. "I'm pleased to have you here. Thank you."

Captain Spiers led them through the ceremony. As he recited the final prayer, Ian leaned over to whisper in Anne's ear, "You've got me into a lot of scrapes, Anne Grant. But this..."

She flashed him a quick grin, and he kissed her.

Captain Spiers shook Ian's hand. He held Anne by the shoulders for a moment, looking into her eyes. Anne was afraid for a moment that he was going to scold her for her wanton deception. Instead, the captain said, "You are a brave lass. I wish you well." Then he gave Anne a kiss on each cheek.

The Sutherlands gave their congratulations, and then the four settlers left the cabin. Not a word was said to any of the other travellers, sparing the young couple nasty gossip and reprimand.

The *Hector* passed St. John Island and beat its way toward Pictou Harbour. There was a buzz of excitement aboard. Land lay all about them. It was only a matter of hours now, and they would be at their destination.

In the morning, Anne sat in the hold with Katherine, watching as each breath laboured in and out of her chest.

"Dear merciful God," Anne prayed, "please let Katherine live. Let her stand on the soil of Nova Scotia. Please let her help her girls and Hugh start their new life in the New World."

Anne bathed Katherine's fevered, pocked brow and hummed bits of hymns to her.

Anne's heart skipped a beat when Katherine's eyes blinked open. Anne whispered, "Katherine?"

Katherine slowly turned her face and focussed her eyes upon Anne. She swallowed loudly.

Anne eased her friend's shoulders up and helped her to sip some water, then lay her gently down again.

Katherine croaked, "The girls."

"Christina is better; she is doing fine now. Elspie has been caring for them all. She has been very good to them."

Katherine gave a slight nod. Then she whispered huskily, "Do not let them throw me in the sea. I want to be buried. On land. Please."

Anne's eyes brimmed with tears. She cradled Katherine's limp fingers in her hands. "Oh Katherine, you will get well now. You…"

Katherine closed her eyes and opened them again. "Nay. Tell Hugh… take good care… the girls. I tried."

Anne squeezed Katherine's frail fingers. "Aye. You are a grand mama to your girls."

Katherine closed her eyes. She took a shuddering breath, then another. And then she breathed no more.

"No," Anne whispered. "Oh no." She lay her head in her arms and wept.

As Anne sobbed bitterly by Katherine's deathbed, the *Hector* slipped into Pictou Harbour.

The great white sails folded like the wings of a giant bird settling; the anchor lowered with a resounding rattle.

The longboat was hoisted from the deck and lowered to the *Hector*'s side.

The settlers on deck cried and laughed in relief. Men rushed to their packs and donned their kilts. They would enter the New World wearing their tartans.

After a time, Anne quietly pulled the blanket up over Katherine's scarred face and shuffled to the ladder. She stared at the *Hector*'s miserable hold for a long moment, then stiffly climbed to the deck.

There was hardly room to walk among the passengers as they milled about, talking and gazing out over the rails. Anne wove through them like a leaf flowing down a stream, not fighting the current but merely edging around obstacles. She finally found Hugh at the starboard bow, with Alexander, Elspie, and their families.

Their animated faces fell when they saw Anne. Her grief was written clearly on her features. Hugh stepped forward and held her hands.

"She is gone?" he asked.

Anne nodded, too sorrowful to speak. Tears filled her eyes again.

Hugh looked to the heavens for a moment, then back at Anne, his eyes moist. "Thank you for caring for her," he whispered. "You're a good friend."

Anne cried, "She spoke, just before she passed. She… she said that she wanted to be buried. On land. Not at sea."

Hugh nodded. "It will be as she asked."

"And she said," Anne choked, "that she tried. And to please take good care of the girls."

Hugh nodded again. He glanced at his girls, playing nearby with their cousins. He lifted both of his hands and swept the tears off his face with his palms.

Alexander stood at his side and said, "They will want for nothing, Hugh."

"That's right," Elspie agreed, coming to his other side and taking Hugh's elbow. "We will help you with the girls. Never fear."

"Thank you. I suppose… I must tell them."

"I will speak to the captain, about arrangements to take her ashore," Alexander said.

Hugh nodded, then took a shuddering breath and made for the children, his shoulders bent. Elspie trailed along to give support.

Anne turned and made for the rail. She slumped against it and gazed out. Having land about seemed foreign after so many weeks of the vastness of the sea. The beach was rocky, and great trees grew down to the shore. Autumn shades of gold and crimson smudged the jade green forest. The air was alive with wheeling birds, squawking and calling to each other. Dark shapes flitted amongst the trees, too quick to make out whether they were human or animal.

John MacKay tuned up his bagpipes and began to play. Master Orr shouted orders to the crew. Passengers gathered their few belongings and waited in hushed anticipation for the longboat to be loaded.

They had arrived. After two and a half months of grueling sea travel, storms, disease, and food shortages, they were here.

Anne hugged her arms about herself. They had gained this shore. But the price!

She gazed mournfully about the deck, her eyes pausing on those who had lost kin during the voyage. Eighteen brave souls died on the *Hector*. How many families would have embarked upon this venture if they could have known?

Hugh sat with Christina and Janet in his lap. Their soft words and sobs carried across the deck. Anne turned her face away.

Anne's gaze paused on Isabel and Jean Fraser, standing by the main mast, their scarred faces hidden in the hoods of their cloaks. They would live out their lives in painful disfigurement. Some of the passengers blamed them for the smallpox deaths, and had shunned them throughout the voyage. Anne pitied them. Surely they couldn't have known they had the illness when they boarded the ship?

Then she spied Janet Fraser, with baby Jane in her arms. She was the breath of new life in all the heartache and death they had suffered. She was like a promise of a future, of something better.

Ian found Anne. He looked very proud, wearing his MacLeod tartan. He took her hand and held it tightly.

They surveyed the shore. Anne thought it did not look so very different from Scotland, except it was wilder, freer, full of possibilities and challenges.

Ian gave her fingers a little squeeze. Anne looked up into his face.

"Well, lass, now it's up to us. To make a life for ourselves here."

Anne took a deep breath of the pine-scented air. "I'm ready, Ian," she said.

Other Quattro Fiction

Texas by Claudio Gaudio
Abundance of the Infinite by Christopher Canniff
The Proxy Bride by Terri Favro
Tea with the Tiger by Nathan Unsworth
A Certain Grace by Binnie Brennan
Life Without by Ken Klonsky
Romancing the Buzzard by Leah Murray
The Lebanese Dishwasher by Sonia Saikaley
Against God by Patrick Senécal
The Ballad of Martin B. by Michael Mirolla
Mahler's Lament by Deborah Kirshner
Surrender by Peter Learn
Constance, Across by Richard Cumyn
In the Mind's Eye by Barbara Ponomareff
The Panic Button by Koom Kankesan
Shrinking Violets by Heidi Greco
Grace by Vanessa Smith
Break Me by Tom Reynolds
Retina Green by Reinhard Filter
Gaze by Keith Cadieux
Tobacco Wars by Paul Seesequasis
The Sea by Amela Marin
Real Gone by Jim Christy
A Gardener on the Moon by Carole Giangrande
Good Evening, Central Laundromat by Jason Heroux
Of All the Ways To Die by Brenda Niskala
The Cousin by John Calabro
Harbour View by Binnie Brennan
The Extraordinary Event of Pia H. by Nicola Vulpe
A Pleasant Vertigo by Egidio Coccimiglio
Wit in Love by Sky Gilbert
The Adventures of Micah Mushmelon by Michael Wex
Room Tone by Gale Zoë Garnett